WINNER TAKES ALL

BY JUDY KENTRUS

WINNER TAKES ALL

Published by Lady K Publishing

Copyright 2015, Lady K, Inc.

Judykentrus.com

CHAPTER 1

"I'm in trouble, so much trouble." Cindi Pearl Sullivan cradled her hot cheeks in her hands. "Do a good deed, for a friend in need," had always been her personal motto, but this time, it was biting her in the ass. "You had to volunteer to take over the financial books for the soap box derby organization. Now a bunch of kids will be heartbroken, especially the Super Kids."

She'd purposely stayed after normal working hours to review the spreadsheets. Lincoln Adams, her boss and owner of Adams Security and Investigations, had left hours ago, wanting to get home to his wife and daughter. Cindi's stomach growled, a reminder that she hadn't eaten anything since lunch. The cafeteria in their new building offered great food and was open twenty-four seven for the convenience of the employees, but the thought of eating made her nauseated.

She moved away from her neatly cluttered desk and took a hesitant step into the deserted corridor of the third floor administrative level. The other two floors were occupied twenty-four hours a day by service representatives and staff who oversaw the monitoring of residential and commercial security systems.

The overwhelming silence was interrupted by the sound of a vacuum cleaner. Before she could step back inside her office, Harriett, the woman from Mary Maids Cleaning Services, exited the office next door. Alexis Long, Lincoln's best friend's wife and owner of Mary Maids, had decided to expand her area of commercial cleaning.

The dark-haired woman, dressed in neat denim coveralls and a light blue shirt, wrapped the cord around her upright machine. "You're working late. So is Mr. Reynolds."

The woman had just confirmed what Cindi suspected. Their top-notch forensic accountant never left on time, as was his habit.

Cindi returned the woman's friendly smile. "I'm trying to catch up on some derby business."

At the mention of the derby, excitement filled her pretty blue eyes. "Alan, my eight-year-old, is so happy about the new derby track. My husband ordered the kit, and they are both working on the car. Mary Maids will be his sponsor."

"Sounds like something Alexis would do."

"Everyone is saying this track was your idea."

Cindi shook her head. "I can't take all the credit. The vacant property belongs to Mr. Adams. I just put the bug in his ear."

Harriet took a step closer to Cindi and placed the tips of her fingers on her arm. "I would personally like to thank you. We've been concerned because Alan was spending too much time in his room. My parents gave him a computer for Christmas and all Alan wants to do is play games. This project was a God send, and has brought my husband and son closer together."

"I'm so glad things are working out for your family."

"Is it okay if I start on Mr. Adams's office? I'll keep the door closed so you won't be disturbed."

"Go right ahead. I don't plan to work too much longer."

As soon as Harriett entered Lincoln's office, Cindi sat in one of the shiny visitor's chairs in front of her desk. Whereas all the other offices had been painted beige, Lincoln indulged his assistant and had the walls painted a light orchid, her favorite color. She reached for the purple-and-pink Slinky on the corner of her desk and flipped it from hand to hand. Her guilty conscience stepped in. "You have no one to blame but yourself. If you hadn't developed Montezuma's revenge of the mouth, you wouldn't be suffering pangs of guilt." She slid the Slinky on her arm like a bangle bracelet, as last Friday night's debacle filled her mind.

Lincoln had reserved the banquet room in the back of Delancy's, the local bar and roadhouse. The party was to celebrate his wife's promotion to lieutenant on the Laurel Heights police force. It appeared half the town was in attendance, all wanting to congratulate Jessie. The food and drink were plentiful and the DJ's upbeat selection of songs had everyone stomping on the hardwood floor. The joint was literally jumping.

Cindi sat between Sallie Mae and Lisa Kay at one of the round tables and tapped her foot. She loved to dance and partners were plentiful, but there was someone she really wanted to dance with. From the moment he'd walked in, her eyes and those of half the women at the party, married or single, settled on his very handsome face. The sharp crease in the front of his black dress trousers called attention to the shine on his custom-made black shoes. The other men were in casual shirts and jeans, but he still wore a white dress shirt, open at the neck. At least he'd removed his silk tie. His dark brown hair was military short on the sides, but the top was longer, and few strands grazed his forehead, drawing attention to his clean-shaven face. She'd never envisioned a guy in nerdy, dark-framed glasses as inviting, but he dripped with sex appeal.

She'd been drawn to Preston Reynolds from the moment he'd shown up for his first interview at their Manhattan office three years ago. Over time, those feelings had grown and turned into something so much stronger. To her delight, she never had to be jealous of other women, because he didn't date. He'd come to the party as an obligation to his boss and very close friend. Preston also stirred up her "Do a good deed, for a friend in need" motto. Psychology had never been her strong point, but in her heart, she understood why he avoided social interaction, especially with the opposite sex. He wore a prosthetic leg from the knee down on his right leg. She wanted to make him understand shying away from relationships and retreating from life was wrong. The Super Kids she worked with in the soap box derby overcame their physical disabilities and participated in the race—and more importantly, life.

He'd taken a seat next to Lincoln and three of their co-workers at Adams Security and politely refused the invitations of women who approached him to dance. It wasn't as if he wasn't capable of physical activity. Lincoln and Preston played racquetball in the corporate gym. He also ran every morning, alone.

When the DJ slowed the beat and started playing James Taylor's "Handy Man," she decided it was time to end his wallflower stigma. She skirted a few couples already on the dance floor and approached Preston with an inviting smile.

"How about a dance?"

Preston sat alone at the table and offered an apologetic smile. "Sorry, Cindi, but I don't dance."

It was the answer she'd expected, but she pressed further. "You mean you don't know how."

"I know how, but I prefer not to dance."

"Why?" Cindi refused to back down.

He noticed a few of the guests at nearby tables were eavesdropping on their conversation, and he tried to remain patient. "You know why."

"No, I don't."

Annoyance laced his light green eyes, and he leaned closer. "I didn't think I would have to spell it out, especially for you."

"Maybe you'd better." She was being a pushy bitch, but didn't care.

He twisted in his seat and lowered his voice. "My leg."

"Is there a problem with your prosthesis?"

"No."

"Then we are back to my original question. Why don't you want to dance?"

He didn't bother to disguise the anger in his voice. "What part of the word *no* don't you understand?"

Cindi's eyes drifted to his large, white-knuckled hands gripped together. That should have been enough of a hint that he was annoyed with her, but she brushed off the warning. "I understand the word perfectly, but you still owe me an explanation."

Until now, he'd avoided looking directly at her. "Let's just say I prefer not making an ass of myself."

"Well, you're too late." Cindi didn't realize the song had ended. Dancers were returning to their seats and inquisitive ears were hanging on her every word. "I don't want to ruin my new purple sandals, so I won't give you a well-deserved kick in said ass. Get over yourself. I've seen kids in wheelchairs that have more courage than you!" When his features paled from her caustic statement, Cindi realized she'd gone too far. Hurting him was the last thing she wanted to do. Fortunately, the DJ dedicated the next song, drawing attention to their guest of honor. Rick Springfield belted out "Jessie's Girl."

"Sorry, Preston," Cindi muttered.

He stood up on two steady feet. "I thought you, of all people, would understand. Bitchiness doesn't become you. I'll say good-night."

The eyes of the other guests registered sympathetic understanding when he left and then turned on Cindi Pearl with cold menace. In the short time Preston had made his home in Laurel Heights, the citizens recognized him as an Army Ranger hero who had been hurt saving Lincoln Adams, one of their own. She'd left shortly after, avoiding her friends. The old song "You Always Hurt the One You Love" was right.

Now she was facing an enormous problem, finding out where one hundred fifty thousand dollars had gone. The foundation fund raiser had netted ten thousand dollars, but Lincoln's generous contribution for the completion of their new soap box track had disappeared. He'd donated the acreage down the road from his new building. The surrounding landscape and lane construction was almost complete.

"Cindi, you called him a coward in front of the whole town, and that's just what you are. You know what has to be done." She'd just put the slinky back on her desk when Harriett exited Lincoln's office.

"Everything is sparkling clean," she said, pulling her dolly cart of cleaning supplies. "Have a good evening."

"I wish," Cindi said for her ears alone. "Move your ass, girl and get it over with." She retrieved her brush from the bottom drawer of her desk and ran it quickly through the tangles in her hair and swiped her lips with pale pink gloss. She was about to leave, but remembered the chocolate chip cookies her roommate had made. "The way to a man's heart is something sweet or a naughty nightie. Prancing into his office in a Victoria's Secret original would surely shake him up, but cookies will have to do."

Preston Reynolds appreciated the surrounding quiet and studied the figures on the wall screen. "Gotcha!" He'd been working on this account for the past week and confirmed insurance fraud to the tune of five million dollars. As a certified forensic accountant, his findings would hold up in any court. He reached for the mug on the corner of his desk and grimaced at his first sip of cold black coffee. Lately, he'd been drinking too much caffeine. The time on the bottom of his computer read nine-fifteen. He'd totally missed dinner. Working after normal business hours was never a problem. In the past seven years, he'd learned to live with the quiet and solitude. It wasn't unusual for him to get lost in the world of figures, something he loved. He was like a dog with a bone, gnawing away at a problem until it was solved. Besides, there wasn't anyone at home waiting for him and never would be. It was hard to ignore the depressing thought.

"Excuse me, Preston."

The soft sound of her voice shattered the silence, and cut right through him. The phrase "get over yourself" flashed through his mind, but the storm of anger he'd suffered over her insensitivity had passed. They'd worked together in Manhattan, their main location, for three years, but he'd been wrestling more and more with the warmhearted feelings he had for sweet, lovely, Cindi Pearl, since he'd moved to the smaller Laurel Heights office. A cramp in his right knee was a tickler he'd been sitting too long and a reminder he wasn't whole. *Keep your distance*, he told himself and swung his chair around.

His heartbeat kicked up at the sight of her standing in his doorway. She'd added lighter highlights to her flaxen-blond hair that barely brushed her shoulders. The flared hem of her zebra-striped dress ended just above her cute knees, revealing slender legs. Deep-orchid-painted toes peeked out from white sandals. He envied the large black-and-white hoop earrings that kissed her peach-hued cheek. "You're working late," he said. He caught the fragrant smell of coffee.

Cindi took hesitant steps into the modern office that was as neat as a pin. Two wall screens and computer stations lined one wall, while his laptop occupied the center of his desk. He'd dimmed the overhead lights and closed the grayish-blue vertical blinds on the tall windows to seal out the night. There was nothing personal in sight.

"You are too," she said and set the cup and clear plastic container of cookies on his desk. "I thought you might like coffee and some of Samantha's homemade chocolate chip cookies."

"You are giving me your favorite cookies?" Preston picked up the white mug and raised it in a sign of thanks, before sipping the hot brew. She knew exactly how he liked his coffee, black and strong.

He had a beautiful mouth, she decided before asking, "How did you know they are my favorite cookie?"

"A little birdie told me that you also love eggplant parmesan and cheesecake. You like to listen to the oldies and volunteer your time at the senior citizens' center."

Cindi ignored the two visitor's chairs and leaned a hip against the corner of his desk. The expected hostility wasn't there, and some of her tension eased. "I'm impressed." Did this mean he was interested in her? Unbeknownst to him, she'd run her own background check on him. At the time, she didn't consider it snooping, just wanting to know a little more about a coworker with a high security clearance. He was thirty-five and his parents lived in Oregon with his sister. Graduating with a degree in accounting, he went into the military and volunteered for the Army Rangers. The information was sparse on how he'd gotten hurt. She watched him take a bite of cookie and sip more coffee. The orchid-and-black pearls around her neck suffered a tug from her nervous fingers. "I owe you a very big apology. The other night, I was heartless and insensitive. I never meant to hurt you. Not wanting to dance was your choice."

Preston set the half eaten cookie on an unused white paper napkin left over from his lunch. "You're absolutely correct."

A wisp of blond hair fell in front of her eye, and his fingers itched to brush it aside and run a finger down her smooth cheek. *Down, boy.*

Cindi inched closer and touched the back of his hand. His skin was smooth and nails neatly trimmed. "I have a tendency to trip on my tongue as well as my feet. I look on you with the highest regard. My cousin is a West Point graduate, and my father was in the Army Reserves. I have a relative who was killed at sea in a training mission for Normandy. You are a hero." Cindi was babbling like a devoted fan, wishing she could confess her true feelings.

He linked their fingers and gave her hand a reassuring squeeze. "I am not a hero, and if I had wanted to dance, it would have been with you."

The sincerity in his voice caressed her like a velvet glove. "So, no hard feelings?"

"None." He reluctantly released her slender hand and held out the container. "Have a cookie."

Relief swamped her body, but she wasn't done. "I had another reason for coming in, not that apologizing wasn't important." Cindi reached into the side pocket of her dress and withdrew a small flash drive. "I'm on the board for our local soap box derby. Thanks to Lincoln and his generous donation of acreage down the road from our building, Laurel Heights will be getting their own track. We had a fund raiser, and Lincoln also donated over a hundred and fifty thousand dollars. The current treasurer had to resign due to health reasons, so I volunteered to take over her financial duties." She passed him the small drive. "I'm not a financial genius, but I'm pretty sure one hundred fifty thousand dollars is missing."

CHAPTER 2

Cindi perched on the corner of Preston's desk when he slipped the drive into an external USB port. "I took over the treasurer's position as a favor to the woman who has handled the finances for many years."

A series of spreadsheets filled one of the wall screens. Preston gave them a cursory inspection and pursed his lips. "These records go back thirty years."

"This particular chapter was started by a group of Vietnam veterans wanting to do something for kids. When the original founders passed away, many of the volunteers faded into the woods, and there weren't enough volunteers to keep the chapter going. Ten years ago, the affiliation was given new life when they received a huge donation. We've been able to have one race a year, closing down a street with the cooperation of the township."

"So you grew up around here?" Along with her likes and social activities, he knew quite a bit about her background, but preferred to keep that to himself.

"My parents still have a house in Stevensville, and my brother is on the local and national derby boards. Even when I lived in Manhattan, I volunteered to do computer work and help out the day of the race. Because of Lincoln's donation, Laurel Heights will be able to sponsor events on their own track."

Preston used a laser pointer to denote a specific amount. "Here is the initial deposit from Adams Security and Investigations. Are you sure it hasn't been disbursed?"

"I double-checked all the way back to the donation. The money is distributed in increments as the construction progresses. Lincoln personally covered the cost of clearing the land and lane paving. The custom arched marquee has been ordered, and the company has requested partial payment. The four sets of bleachers are sixty-four thousand dollars." Cindi sighed deeply. "The ledger columns appear to balance, but someone's been playing tic-tac-toe with the funds."

"Do you know if the organization ever experienced money problems in the past?"

"If it did, I'm sure my brother would have mentioned it to me."

Preston scrolled through a few more spreadsheets and stopped. "What is this numbered account? 4-15-12-16-8-9-14."

Cindi had just bitten into a cookie and chewed quickly. "Every year we receive a stipend from a secret benefactor. A number of kids live in foster care and wouldn't be able to participate without this person's donation. The money covers the cost of their cars, transportation to the event—basically all of their expenses."

"So you don't know the identity of this person?"

"Don't have a clue. I do know it isn't Lincoln."

"I'll see what I can find out about your mysterious philanthropist. Who can sign off on expenditures?"

"Two signatures are required on all checks—the president of the board and the treasurer who just resigned. And now me."

He momentarily glanced away from the figures, and his eyes were drawn to a pair of beautiful slender legs. She'd crossed her knees and the edge of her skirt had ridden up, exposing shapely thighs. *How would they feel wreathed around his hips? Stop torturing yourself,* he told himself and forced his attention back to the problem at hand. "As part of my investigation, I'll need to look into the financial status of all the board members."

"I was afraid you were going to say that. I've got nothing to hide and neither does my brother, but I am very uncomfortable invading the other members' privacy. Let's see what you can uncover going over the accounts."

"It's against procedure, but we'll try it your way, for now."

The silence lingered in the office, and Cindi savored this time with Preston, appreciating how his green eyes, shielded by his nerdy glasses, seem to absorb the figures on the spreadsheets. Every once in a while, he would make a note on the yellow pad on his desk and then return to the accounts. The growl from her stomach broke the silence. "Pardon me," she said, clamping an arm about her waist. "I never did get to eat dinner."

Preston shifted away from the wall screen and gave her a small smile of understanding. "Me either. I finished the Morgan investigation. The insurance company is going to love us when then don't have to pay out all that money. I'll work on your project tomorrow after I get back from Manhattan." He looked at his watch. "It's after ten, and I have to be back here at seven to meet the company helicopter."

"I forgot that you are helping the boss interview applicants for your counterpart in the Manhattan office. I know Lincoln will be flying with you, but please don't mention this situation. Let's see if we can find out what happened to the money first."

Preston arched a brow at her request. One did not hold back from their boss. He copied the files to his laptop and passed the drive back to Cindi.

"Thanks" she said and returned it to her pocket. "How can I repay you for helping?"

Sometimes luck just fell into one's lap, like now. He raised his eyes to the ceiling and offered a silent thank-you. He'd debated approaching Cindi to help him with a problem he was facing later in the week. He needed a date, and she would understand things wouldn't go any further than a friendly evening. "Have dinner with me."

Cindi never expected him to ask her out, not after the other night. "I'd love to. What night did you have in mind?" she quickly asked. *Pushy, pushy, slow down girl.* Other than her volunteering obligations, her calendar was wide open.

He'd heard the eagerness in her voice, and tried to let her down gently. "I'd better explain. My sister Jennifer is coming to Laurel Heights to interview for the directorship of the new community center. It won't be up and running until next year, but they are already looking for staff. I'd like you to join us for dinner."

Her fluttering heart slowed from disappointment. She should have known the invitation was too good to be true. "When was the last time you saw your sister?"

"A year ago, when I went home to visit my parents in Oregon for their thirty-fifth wedding anniversary. Jennifer has her own place a few minutes from them."

"Wouldn't you rather meet with her alone?"

"Not really." He picked up the pen and started to write a nonsensical formula on the yellow pad. *Stop stalling. Tell her the real reason you are inviting her to dinner.* "I better explain. My parents and sister are worried that I am no longer interested in women. Jennifer actually came out and asked if I was gay." Now came the hard part. "I'd like to introduce you as my girlfriend and give her the impression we are lovers."

His words exploded in her brain. Girlfriend! Lover! Is he out of his mind! Cindi tugged on the hem of her dress and hopped off the desk, unaware of the nearby garbage can. The heel of her right shoe penetrated the top of a Styrofoam container that contained a half-eaten egg salad sandwich.

She put a hand to the side of the desk to steady herself and screwed up her face at her klutzy blunder. When she lifted her foot out of the can, the container was still attached to her heel. "Oh, yuck!"

Preston knew enough not to laugh. "Let me help you." He grasped the back of her bare leg to give her support, but his fingers encountered lovely, soft skin. The silky, smooth surface had to be the result of body lotion. Of their own free will, his fingertips slowly caressed the length of her calf and slipped off her white toeless shoe.

Cindi melted the moment he touched the back of her knee, and she forced herself to remain still when his fingers brushed her skin with warm heat. Her entire leg tingled, and spread throughout the rest of her body, from his enticing touch. She could always claim sexual harassment, but she enjoyed it too much.

He purposely turned his back, not wanting her to see his obvious arousal. "Sorry about that," he said, and used his own white handkerchief to clean off her shoe. "I mean the mess in the can," he quickly added and passed her the now clean shoe. He didn't dare pull a glass slipper move. Touching her once was all he could handle.

I'm not, she silently noted as her heartbeat returned to normal. "I'm a klutz. Now, what were you saying about giving your sister the impression we are lovers?" Cindi surprised herself by not getting tongue tied over the word "lover."

"There isn't any other woman I could trust to pull this off. You are a good friend and won't get the wrong idea if I start putting the moves on you in public. I just want to be up-front."

His common sense explanation threw a bucket of ice water on her happiness. She jammed her hands on her hips at the insult. "So I'm just a good ole boy—I mean, girl—you need to pass off as your lover just to prove you aren't into guys!"

"I didn't mean it quite that way. You are a beautiful, warm, sensitive woman any man would be lucky to call his girlfriend or lover." *I would make love to you in a heartbeat, but it's impossible*, he silently added.

Now she was getting angry. "Just so I understand your deceitful, half-ass invitation. If you get touchy-feely and plant a few kisses during dinner, I should react like it's perfectly normal since we're lovers. It would all be for show."

"Absolutely." *God forgive me for lying.*

Cindi tipped her head to the side and decided to toss out a challenge. "You know, it works both ways. I might want to take a few liberties, you know, to make our relationship more convincing. Like you said, it would all be for show."

"No problem. I'll do my part." Maybe this wasn't a good idea, he thought, but it was too late now to take back his invitation.

"Have you considered what might happen if your sister gets the job and comes to live in Laurel Heights?"

"I'll worry about that when and if it happens. We can always say things didn't work out."

Not if I can help it. Momma didn't raise a dummy. She needed to give this situation a little more thought, but held out a hand. "We have a deal. You clean up my financial mess and I'll pretend to be your lover."

Preston wondered at the designing gleam in her eyes, but then decided it was just his imagination. He could trust sweet, sensible Cindi Pearl.

Cindi walked into the back door of the Spoonful Café at seven the following morning. Sleep had been sporadic. The times she did sink into slumber, her dreams were filled with a deliciously naked Preston romping between the paved lanes of a racetrack, holding up a sign that read "Catch me if you can."

The smell of frying bacon permeated the kitchen of the restaurant, which was already hopping since it was the only place open in Laurel Heights serving a down-home breakfast. The sleepy community in the Laurel Highlands of Pennsylvania was currently experiencing a growth spurt. Thanks to Lincoln Adams, a fully equipped community center was under construction.

Sam Morlock owned and oversaw the conversion of two old brick warehouses into spacious condos. His family heritage was in railroading, so he rehabbed the adjacent train station and leased the space to specialty shops. A fourth building was being converted into a train museum. The town was also buzzing with workers putting in natural gas wells on numerous farm properties owned by the town and Lincoln Adams. Previously vacant stores on Main Street had drawn a variety of new retailers.

"You got home late. Was he hot?" asked Samantha Kingsley, Cindi's best friend. Sam plated a Mexican omelet, grilled tomatoes, home fries and bacon and set the oval dish on the shelf next to her workstation and tapped the pickup bell.

He is. "No such luck." Cindi gratefully accepted a cup of coffee from Samantha.Sam was also another newbie to Laurel Heights and had purchased the farmhouse where Cindi lived. A white butcher's apron camouflaged the body of a tall, svelte woman who could pass for a runway model. She'd plaited her champagne-blond hair into a long braid and wrapped her head with a scarf in jewel tones. Until recently, she'd worked for Adams Security. After ten years as an undercover agent, Sam had resigned to fulfill her dream. Tea in Time, a Victorian-themed tea shop and small bakery, would open in a few months.

Cindi accepted a warm carrot-raisin muffin from Samantha, already slathered with honey butter. "I fed the critters. Brownie, Pound Cake's calf, is really thriving. I'm concerned about my pygmy goat. Donut is very attached to the ducks. When Cupcake and Muffin go for a swim in the pond, he jumps in after them. I think of them as the three amigos."

"I love it that our menagerie gets along." Sam grabbed another order sheet from the clips and cracked two eggs on the grill. "So, what had you working late?"

"Soap box derby stuff."

Samantha didn't need a crystal ball to sense there was something off with her friend, who was normally upbeat and full of life. Unfortunately, Cindi Pearl was always in hurry and had a tendency to walk into things. "Do I need a crowbar to pry it out of you? We've known each other for ten years, and you've got trouble written all over your face." Sam raised a dark blond brow. "You're not even wearing something purple."

Lifting the weight of this problem off her shoulders would help, and Sam could be trusted. "This is between us. It's about—" Cindi stopped when the kitchen door opened.Sallie Mae Whipper, owner of the Spoonful Café, walked in, carrying a round tray of dirty dishes. She was in her usual black-and-white check pants and pristine white blouse. The ties on her scalloped red apron barely reached around her full form to create a neat bow. White swirls blended with her corkscrew black hair. Her chocolate-brown skin glowed with vitality, but she admitted her bones were getting tired.

"It's so busy out there, you would think we are giving the food away. Morn'n, Cindi Pearl," Sallie Mae greeted her, setting the tray on the stainless steel shelf next to the commercial dishwasher. "My, you look pretty in pink. Lose your way to Lincoln's new building?"

Cindi accepted the warm hug. "Just wanted to check in with Sam."

"I hear Preston Reynolds's sister is interviewing for the directorship of the community center."

"You know about Jennifer already? I only found out last night." If anyone knew what was going on in Laurel Heights, it was Sallie Mae. She was also known as the keeper of secrets.

"Lincoln asked me to sit on the board for the new community center, so I'm fully aware of the candidates. I'd better get out there and spell my servers. Don't want to miss any gossip." Sallie grinned.

Three waitresses hurried in and attached their slips to the clips before picking up their food orders. Cindi's chance to have a private talk with Samantha wasn't about to happen. "I'll talk to you this evening."

She barely had time to think when she got to work. Lincoln had intended to gradually build up their security installation and design division in the rural area, but they had more business than they could handle due to his stellar reputation in the industry. She was disappointed there wasn't a note or e-mail from Preston. He'd never told her what evening his sister would be in town.

She was just about to leave the office for the day when Lincoln sent a priority e-mail listing what to expect in his absence and video meetings he would be conducting the next two days with their offices in Chicago and Los Angeles. She shook her head and laughed. It was the same information she'd sent him that morning. Ever since he'd found out Jessie was going to have a baby, he'd taken on the persona of a very nervous expectant father.

After dinner, Cindi relaxed in one of the rocking chairs on the side porch with her iPad in her lap. The midsummer sky was filled with thousands of stars, and the sweet scent from the French lilacs that framed the roofline perfumed the air. A slight breeze ruffled the tall cornstalks in the neighboring fields, and the humid heat clung to her skin. She liked the sound that the crickets made when they rubbed their back legs together.

Her heart beat a little faster when she read the e-mail from Preston. *Cindi, due to follow-up interviews, I'll be in the New York office another two days. Jennie's meeting with the board of directors is on Friday afternoon and dinner will be Friday evening. Please make a seven o'clock reservation at the Laurel Bistro. Thank you, Preston.* "Wow, you are going all out." New owners had purchased the double storefront and turned it into a popular five-star restaurant. The married couple adhered to the town's strict guidelines to keep the antique integrity on the interior. The down-home citizens had suffered culture shock from the pricey fare, but rumor had it the cuisine was outstanding. Getting a reservation was going to be a challenge.

Samantha nudged the screen door open with her hip and set a small tray on the table between the rockers. "I thought you might like a glass of sweet tea. Chores are done and critters are down for the night. While you are telling me what's bothering you, try out those mini scones. It's a new recipe. I've laced them with cinnamon bits, apples and cranberries."

Cindi had just placed her iPad on the table when a firefly landed on the back of her hand. "Hi there," she laughed, watching his yellow flashing glow. "When I was a little girl, my brother and I would collect lightning bugs and put them in a jar. My dad punched holes in the lids so they could breathe. We left them in the jar when we went to bed. In the morning, the bugs were gone and we always believed lightning bugs had magic powers. It wasn't until we were a little older that my mother admitted to setting them free."

"I love hearing about your childhood, but you're stalling."

Cindi reached for a scone and placed it on a lacy white napkin. "All right, here it is. I took over the books for our local soap box derby chapter, and there is a hundred and fifty thousand dollars missing. Preston asked me out to dinner with his sister, but wants me to pretend to be his lover because his parents and sister think he's gay."

Samantha's mouth dropped. "Oh shit!"

CHAPTER 3

"How do you get into these things? That is a lot of missing money. Stealing from kids is just plain evil. As for Preston's dinner invitation, who does he think he is, using you that way?"

Cindi bit into the scone and shrugged a shoulder. "We have an agreement. He helps me with my money problem, and I go to dinner with him, pretending to be his lover." She took another bite, chewed slowly and nodded. "These are a winner. I like the sugar coating on the outside. You don't even need clotted cream."

"So noted. I'm glad you like them. As for your problem, it's a bullshit agreement. You are deceiving his sister, and it's a personal insult to you." Sam grabbed her braid and twirled around the paintbrush end like a feather boa. Merriment filled her eyes. "It would serve him right if you showed up doing your ditzy blonde impersonation."

Cindi's eyes widened at the horrible suggestion. "I couldn't do that. Suppose he gets pissed and changes his mind about helping me? I could be arrested for embezzlement. On top of that, his sister might think I'm a real dingbat."

"You would definitely shake up his boring self, but I don't think he'd go back on his word. He's too stiff and honorable."

Samantha studied the indecision on Cindi's face. "What else haven't you told me? Better yet, how do you really feel about Preston Reynolds?"

Donut, Cupcake and Muffin chose that moment to escape the barn and join the party on the porch. The ducks quacked twice and circled Samantha's chair before settling at her feet. Donut hopped up on Cindi's lap and nuzzled his way into her arms.

"Party crashers," Cindi laughed softly and hugged him closer, nuzzling his black-and-white furry neck. "I love Preston, but he doesn't love himself. He's personable and friendly to everyone, but inside, I sense he's given up and retreats from the world he knew before he got hurt. I want to shake him and make him realize it's not the end. He is alive and life is worth living."

"I'm sorry I missed the fiasco the other night. You had already left the party when I arrived. The room was abuzz with you and Preston."

"He only showed up out of respect for Lincoln and Jessie. I had good intentions, but as usual, my tongue worked faster than my brain. I've apologized for embarrassing him in front of the guests and half the town. 'Think before you act' should become my new personal motto."

"I understand where you are coming from, because you are a determined, caring and generous person. When it comes to Preston, those feelings are much stronger. Doing something for the one you love is more of a challenge, especially when it meets with stubborn resistance. It's going to take hard work and time before he realizes you know what's good for him. So, you're going to show up for dinner as sweet Cindi Pearl?"

"Looks that way."

"You're a better woman than I am. If you change your mind, I've got the perfect dress upstairs. I wore it during an undercover operation as a hooker."

"If I change my mind, I'll let you know."

Late Thursday morning, Cindi finally got a chance to sort through the mail on her desk. Lincoln's first day back in the office had her busier than normal. Right now, he was in a closed-door meeting with Treig Taylor, one of their undercover agents, discussing a new assignment. She needed to talk to Preston about their dinner reservation tomorrow night and decided it could wait until she finished reviewing the correspondence. A half dozen FedEx boxes were stacked on the floor next to her desk. Her eyes kept drifting to the one on the top, addressed to Cindi Pearl personally. The return address was from a toy manufacturer in California. "I didn't order anything." Curiosity was eating away at her patience. "The rest of the mail can wait."

She retrieved a slim cutter from the top drawer in her desk and slit the clear tape, but encountered another sealed package. A plain white gift card had been taped to the top. The big smile on her face dimmed when she read the message. *If you don't back off, this could happen, for real.* She ignored standard security precautions and eagerly lifted out the smaller box. In her haste to open the lid, the sharp tip of the cutter caught the edge of her finger, drawing blood. "Nice job, Cindi Pearl," she chastised herself, thrusting her bleeding finger in her mouth and continued to dig for the contents with her other hand. A rusty taste coated her tongue, but the blood drained from all her features at the sight of a black, white and gray stuffed animal, a replica of her dear, sweet Donut. Tears ran unheeded down her paled cheeks when she lifted the fluffy critter out of the bubble packing. The pigmy goat's neck had been twisted and drooped at an unnatural angle.

The door to Lincoln's office opened and he walked out smiling, along with Treig. Both paused at the sight of tears running down Cindi's face and the mangled stuffed animal in her hand.

Treig rushed over to Cindi. "What the hell! That critter could pass for Donut. What bastard could be so heartless?" He removed the toy from her shaking hand and set it on the desk. "Come here, baby doll," he crooned and gathered her in.

Cindi buried her face in his strong shoulder and wrapped her arms around his slim body. A stream of hot tears dripped onto his button-down shirt. Treig was a good friend, and they'd dated on and off. Settling down with one woman was in the far future for him. He'd almost lost his life a few months ago working undercover for Pennsylvania's Alcoholic Beverage Control and just started working for Adams Security. Treig wasn't ready to visit St. Peter. Life meant having fun and taking a few risks.

Lincoln ignored his brother-in-law's cuddling of his admin and picked up the stuffed animal. He would have liked to twist the neck of the person who'd been so cruel to Cindi. He, Jessie and Edie had been with Cindi when she picked out the little goat. His ten-year-old daughter decided a pigmy goat would be a great addition to their growing family. Lincoln promised if and when they moved to a farm, she could have one. Edie had been less than satisfied with his answer.

Momentary panic set in, and Cindi jerked her head up, whacking Treig on his chin. "Oh, my God! How does this person know about Donut? That means he knows where I live! Suppose he went to the farm, for real! Sam is still at the Spoonful!"

Treig wiggled his jaw and rubbed his sore chin. "I'll go to the farm right now."

The thought had already occurred to Lincoln. "Wait, I've got a better idea." He took out his cell phone and retrieved the number he used quite frequently. He put the call on speakerphone and it was picked up on the second ring.

"Clyde's Gardening Service, Clyde speaking. How ya doin', Mr. Adams?"

"Just the man I need." Lincoln said. "Can you do me a solid right away and go over to Samantha Kingsley's farm and make sure the animals are okay?"

"I left there ten minutes ago and everything was fine. At first I couldn't find Donut, but he was jumping in the lake. Can't understand it. Goats don't like going in water. He is such a rascal. I started on the lawn in the front of the house and he leaped on my shoulders. Stayed there the entire time and did his rendition of shake, rattle and roll. I'm still wet. Is there a problem, Mr. Adams?"

"Not anymore. Thanks, Clyde." Lincoln reached for a tissue from the box on her desk and held it out. "You heard him. The animals are fine. Wipe and blow. Then you had better tell me what's going on."

Cindi gratefully accepted the tissue and wiped the lingering wetness from her cheeks. "Maybe I'd better."

Preston read over the report, satisfied he'd gone as far as he could in his investigation of a computer company misrepresenting their earnings in anticipation of selling the company. He e-mailed his findings to their fraud department, but he needed to talk to Lincoln about a pending investigation. The priority report had taken longer than anticipated, and he hadn't been able to research Cindi Pearl's problem. He unrolled the sleeves of his white dress shirt and reached for his sports from the back of his chair. Before leaving, he grabbed his cane, a gift from the physical therapist that had helped Preston through a hellish period in his life. As he walked down the wide, carpeted corridor on his way to Lincoln's office, he returned friendly waves. The staff in Manhattan had been cordial, but his new coworkers drew him into their fold liked he'd been born and raised in the Highlands. A number of men and women had transferred from other offices, but the team Lincoln had formed blended with ease and efficiency. He was appreciative of the invitations to join them in a night of bowling, drinks or dinner after work, but he was still trying to find his groove.

He'd felt too confined by the tall buildings in the city. Having grown up in Oregon, he loved living in the wide open spaces. He liked that he could look out the wide windows at the surrounding mountains. The pines, maples and oaks were a rich, vibrant green, flourishing under the sun's summer warmth. They would look magnificent in the fall.

Hearing voices, he paused in the doorway to Cindi's office. His body stiffened like cold, hard steel and his fingers gripped the arch of his cane. Cindi was being clasped tightly in the arms of Treig John Taylor. What hurt even more, she was returning his embrace! The green-eyed monster double-punched him in the gut. He had no right to harbor these feelings of jealousy. In reality, he could never give her what she needed. It was torture and he needed to leave. His tongue felt thick, and he barely got the words out.

"Excuse me. I didn't mean to interrupt. I'll come back later." He abruptly turned about and ignored Lincoln's request to wait. Jealous resentment continued to burn in his body, and he almost stumbled in his haste to return to the privacy of his office. He stepped inside, and closed the door firmly. "Goddamn it!" he raved. Not giving any thought to his action, the cane in his hand became an onyx lance. It flew across the room, just missing one of the wall screens, and plummeted to the dark gray carpeting. He was shocked at the intensity of his anger and pain, especially around his heart.

"Where the hell did that come from?" he muttered, sitting in the padded armchair behind his desk. His hands were still trembling. Seeing the woman he loved in the arms of another man had triggered an intense reaction he hadn't felt in years, a time before he lost his leg. The pain around his heart was a reminder he couldn't tell her how he felt. He wasn't whole. Treig was a great guy and could give her love, physical pleasure, everything she needed from a man. "Shit! Shit! Shit!"

Treig refused to leave and held Cindi's hand while she confessed all. Lincoln leaned against his desk and asked very few questions until she was finished.

"Cindi Pearl Sullivan. Why am I not surprised you were going to try and solve this on your own? At least you had enough sense to consult Preston. Whoever sent you that stuffed animal isn't playing games. The amount of missing money means this isn't just a penny ante theft. This is grand larceny, and we have to notify the police."

"Not yet, please!" Cindi shoved away from Treig, this time being careful not to injure his sore chin, and transferred her grip to Lincoln's arm. "Can't we keep the theft in-house? If it got out, our volunteers and supporters would cut us off at the knees. It would also damage the reputation of the entire derby community. It's hard enough getting donations. You've got better resources and equipment than the Laurel Heights and state police combined. Not all of our chapters have a superhero named Lincoln Adams."

"I'm not a superhero. Your reasoning is sound, but I'm going to tell Jessie. That way, we will be officially notifying the police. I will also set up a separate account to cover expenses until we find out who took the original hundred and fifty thousand dollars. We'll start back tracking the package while Preston investigates the financial end. We can have our private lab dust for prints, but the perp probably used gloves, and the outer package passed through too many hands."

"Oh, thank you, thank you, boss! I bless the day I walked into you with my hot latte."

"Me too, Cindi Pearl," Lincoln laughed. "Edie plans to run in the stock category. If I went home and told her the race is going to be postponed indefinitely, I might lose my happy home. Knowing her, she'd want to start a 'Save the Race' campaign. I also don't want to disappoint the other kids, especially the Super Kids."

"I wish I could help you out," Treig said, "but our boss just gave me an undercover assignment."

Cindi had full knowledge of where TJ was going and what the job entailed. "You be careful. This is serious. No heroics, but get that bastard," she said, and gave him a warm hug.

He kissed her on the forehead. "I will, doll face, and don't forget to put a Band-Aid on your finger."

When she got back to her desk, the stuffed animal had been removed. Looking at the poor critter made her think too much of Donut. She also felt a great deal better knowing she could cover the derby expenses, and they wouldn't lose their funding or disappoint the children.

It was already after four, and she needed to talk to Preston so they could finalize their plans for the following night. She stopped in the break room to get two cups of coffee, but paused outside his door when she heard him talking to someone on his cell. Not wanting to interrupt his conversation, she waited in the corridor.

"The Last Chance Motel isn't five-star, but it's clean. I'll pick you up at six-thirty tomorrow night."

Cindi's ears perked up when he mentioned the following evening. *Wrong, wrong, wrong,* she told herself, but the female curiosity imbedded in every woman told her to listen.

"No, I'm not getting married. She's no one special, just a casual friend. We get it on from time to time, just to relieve the sexual tension. Neither of us is attached."

No one special! Casual friend! Sexual tension! Cindi silently fumed when there was a pause in his conversation.

"What do you mean I'm being evasive? She's a woman and pees the same way you do! We work for Adams Security, but keep our relationship quiet. I'm not lying! She isn't a hooker I hired for the evening."

"That's it!" Angry footsteps carried her back to her office. "I'll show you 'no one special.'" She drank both cups of now tepid coffee, wishing they were laced with a shot of Kahlúa, pulled out her cell phone and left a message. "Samantha, you know that dress you told me about? Well, dig it out of the mothballs. Preston Reynolds has a date with a hooker tomorrow night."

She made a second call to Jojo's Curl Up n Dye, the full-service salon that opened on Main Street a few months ago. "Jojo, I have an emergency. I need a pedicure and a full set of tips. Can you fit me in on my lunch hour tomorrow? Make sure you have a good supply of neon pink nail polish. Oh, and I'll want one of those temp tattoos you've been advertising. Twelve-thirty, great. Thanks, Jojo."

She hung up and spouted. "No one special! Tomorrow night you'll find out exactly how special I am!"

CHAPTER 4

"Do you think she'll like me?" Jennie Reynolds adjusted the knot at the back of her head, making sure none of the hair had come loose. She'd hated confining her honey-blond hair, but she'd wanted to make a good impression on the committee and her brother's date. The gray business suit and neat hair portrayed her as a professional woman for her interview. For luck, she'd worn her pin in the shape of a soccer ball, a gift from a grateful group of teens she'd coached and won a state championship. It made her sad to think her coaching days were over, but she really wanted this job and all the challenges it entailed. After dinner, she planned to go for a run to burn off the calories from their fancy meal.

Preston checked his watch, wondering what was keeping Cindi Pearl. The reservation was for seven, and she was already ten minutes late. Having dinner with Cindi in the popular restaurant would raise a few eyebrows and feed the gossip hounds, but they were coworkers and his sister was present, so it wouldn't appear as if they were actually on a date.

Every table in the richly decorated dining room was filled. He appreciated that the owners had retained the age-old character, right down to the nineteenth-century, tin ceilings. They'd matched the dark cherry wood dining tables to the wainscoted walls.

Jennie watched her brother finger the black crystals that dripped from the rim of the bell-shaped lampshade on the short bronze lamp in the center of the table. "Hey, Preston James. Stop your wool gathering and answer my question. Do you think she'll like me?"

"Jennifer, you don't have to impress Cindi."

"Stop calling me that. Only mother and father use that name when they are annoyed with me."

"Okay, Jen. She is a very nice woman I work with." Preston sipped ice water from a short-stemmed glass, hoping they could successfully pull off this charade and not have it come back and bite him in the ass. They just had to get through this evening, and his sister would go home with the knowledge he was still interested in women.

The waiter, dressed in a formal black tuxedo, approached their table. "Can I get you something from the bar while you're waiting for your other guest?"

"We'll both have Cutty Sark and water, three cubes."

"It's nice to know you remember what I drink." Her brother's unease was obvious. He kept adjusting the perfect knot in his silk tie and checking his watch. He could have modeled for *GQ* magazine with his excellent taste in clothes, but Preston was such a tight-ass and should have learned to relax. What had happened to the carefree hell-raiser she grew up with and drove their parents crazy? She couldn't remember the last time she saw him smile or heard his hearty laugh. "Tell me more about your lady love. Is she your age?"

"She is not my lady love, and to be perfectly honest, I don't know how old she is, probably younger than me. I met her three years ago when I started working at the Manhattan location for Adams Security. I'm positive you'll like her."

"Was she the reason you transferred to Laurel Heights?"

"No, don't be ridiculous!"

"And he blushes!" Devilment danced in Jennie's light green eyes, the same color as her brother's. "I called Mom and told her you had a girlfriend."

His sister loved to bust his chops, and he summoned all the patience in his body. "Cindi's not a girlfriend, just an occasional lover. Mom's probably planning the damn wedding!"

"Not quite. Just the bridal shower," she teased, and patted the back of his hand. "Don't sweat it, baby brother. They want grandchildren and it's all up to you. I'll be forty in a few months and don't plan to start changing diapers this late in life. You can't raise a kid on Social Security. Don't get me wrong, I like men, but I don't need one to tell me what to do and how to run my life." Jennie turned serious and flattened her hand on his chest, directly over his heart. "It's just us, so be honest. What happened to Dolphin, the devil-may-care boy who lived in here?"

No one had referred to him by his nickname in a long time. Growing up, he could never bullshit his older sister because she always understood and read into him. "He died seven years ago. Life as I knew it is gone forever." He offered a small, tight-lipped smile and captured her hand. "I have a ten-figure bank account and a great job with lots of friends. I'm content."

"But are you happy?"

Preston was relieved the server chose that moment to deliver their drinks. Jen would be able to tell if he lied.

The waiter glanced at the vacant seat. "Would you like to order an appetizer or wait for your other guest?"

"She'll be here soon," he replied before raising his glass to his sister. "Hope you get the job. Laurel Heights is a great place to live, and it will be nice having you around."

"Thanks. Me, too. I really need a change of atmosphere after the scandal.

"You had nothing to do with the misappropriation of funds."

"I know that and I was totally upfront with the committee this afternoon since they plan to run the Norman Taylor Community Center as a nonprofit foundation. I'd have the upper hand in deciding what athletic programs that would be offered so more people will benefit from the amenities, especially those with physical impairments." Jen helped herself to a piece of warm sourdough bread from the small cutting board the server had just placed on the table and reached for a pat of butter shaped like a sunflower. "You know, Mom and Dad were disappointed you didn't come home after you left rehab. They had planned a big party to honor your heroism. Dad was going to approach the Mayor to give you a plaque."

He tightened his fingers around the sweating glass. "When are you and the rest of the world going to understand, I am not a hero? It's been seven years. They act like it was yesterday. That's the first thing Mom brings up every time I come home, followed by asking when am I going to find a nice girl and settle down."

Preston noticed the maître d' had just escorted an attractive couple to a table on the other side of the dining room. "If you need proof Cindi is a coworker, my boss and his wife just came in."

"I had the pleasure of meeting that gorgeous hunk this afternoon. With his black hair in a queue and that black eye patch, he looks like a pirate. I'd become his willing captive anytime. I'd even let him tie me up."

"You did hear me say the beautiful woman with the reddish-gold hair, holding Lincoln's hand, is his wife? I'd be very careful if I were you. She might be the one capturing you for trying to mess with her man. She carries a gun."

"Gun?"

"She's a lieutenant on the Laurel Heights police force."

Preston was getting anxious and pushed back the sleeve of his navy blazer. The time on his gold watch said seven-twenty. What was keeping Cindi?

"I am out of my freakin' mind." Cindi managed to squeeze Pansy, her VW Beetle, into one of the few vacant parking spaces on Main Street. Before the infusion of new stores, the center of town had been practically dead when the sun went down. "I'd be better off at home, snuggled up with Donut on the love seat in my bedroom, watching reruns of *Lavern & Shirley*."

A softly lighted banner of Tiffany glass panels framed the expansive front window and a variety of decorative dwarf trees wasn't enough to hide the intimate dining room. Her anxiety increased when she noticed that all of the linen-draped tables were occupied. Before reaching for the brass door handle, she glanced down to check the bodice on her halter dress. Samantha's boobs were bigger, and Cindi had stuffed a couple of socks in the bodice so her breasts appeared fuller. Her feet throbbed like a toothache. She'd had to borrow skinny strap stilettos that were too small. She'd be lucky if she didn't break an ankle.

She pulled open one of the wood-framed glass doors and stepped into a small vestibule. A maître d', formally dressed in a black-tie tuxedo, stood before a concierge podium and greeted three other couples. His head of thick, snow-white hair was neatly trimmed, as was his handlebar moustache. She swayed nervously from side to side and hummed along with the softly playing instrumental version of "Memory" that filled the richly decorated space.

"Good evening, madam. May I help you?"

Cindi stepped up the podium and purposely kept her voice low. His engraved nametag, just below the fresh white rosebud in his lapel, read "Simmons". "I don't normally dress like this, Simmons, but I'm playing a joke on a friend. I'm a really nice person. I run the bingo games at the senior citizens' center, and go to church every Sunday." Cindi leaned in a bit closer. "The tat on my arm isn't permanent."

"It's quite all right," he replied with an understanding smile. "The name of your party?

"Preston Reynolds."

"He is already seated. Follow me."

The moment they stepped into the dining room, conversation, eating and drinking stopped. All the eyes of the well-dressed diners zeroed in on the blonde bombshell in hot pink.

Lincoln just happened to glance away from the leather-bound menu in his hand and blinked once, twice, telling himself the hussy in the flashy pink dress, with the exaggerated, hip-swinging walk, wasn't his Cindi Pearl headed for the table occupied by his forensic accountant.

Jessie had just decided on the surf and turf and turned her head to ask Lincoln what he wanted to eat, but followed his gaze. Her mouth dropped. "Oh my God, tell me that isn't your sweet, wonderful assistant."

"I wish I could," he chuckled. "My gut is telling me we are about to get a floor show with our dinner. We may live in a small town, but things are far from dull."

"The other night, I got the impression they didn't like one another."

Lincoln settled his eyes on his beautiful wife, who was carrying his son or daughter. "I wish you could have known him before he got hurt. He's done an about-face in the personality department. We were in the same Army Ranger unit, and there wasn't anything he wouldn't do or try. He was a damn explosives specialist. I wouldn't be sitting here if it wasn't for him."

Jessie leaned forward and kissed her husband softly. "Remind me to thank him for making sure you weren't killed. As for Cindi, aren't you going to do something?"

"Not at this time. I think she has got him by the proverbial—excuse the expression—balls, and is about to give him a run for his money. She is exactly what he needs."

"How do you think he'll react to the ceremony tomorrow night? Have you invited him?"

"With all that has been going on this past week, it slipped my mind."

An idea formed in Jessie's head. "Leave it to me."

Preston was oblivious to the hand-shielded whispers from the other diners and unaware his dinner date had arrived until the maître d' approached his chair.

"Sir, your other guest has arrived."

Preston sighed with relief, pushed his chair back and stood up. The welcoming smile on his face dimmed and he closed his eyes, wondering if he imagined the gaudy vision before his eyes. "Cindi?" he choked out.

"Hi, honeybunch." Her voice was thick with the ditzy blonde routine she was putting on. "Sorry I'm late. I had a pair of sheer silk stockings that I wanted to wear because I know how much you like to feel up my legs, but I accidentally poked a hole in the material with my nails." Cindi wiggled the long, shocking-pink nail extensions and then raised the hem of her dress a good four inches above her knees. "See, my legs are bare naked."

She twirled around like a glittery spinning top and grabbed his shoulder when her ankle started to give way. The furious look on his face said her plan was working.

"Hope you don't think my dress is too sparkly." She dipped her head to the side and pouted. "I'm really sorry about the green streaks in my hair. It was supposed to come out pink like my dress, but something went really wrong. I wanted to look nice for your sister." She ran a hand down the front of his rose-and-cream-colored tie. "Aw, that is so sweet. How did you know

I was going to wear pink? You can tie me up later and I'll add it to my collection of your silk ties. Oops," she giggled, "I probably won't be wearing anything."

Jennie, too, was at a loss for words and wondered if this woman was for real. She was enjoying the show much too much. "Since my brother has turned mute, I'll introduce myself." She held out a hand. "Jennifer Reynolds, but I prefer Jen or Jennie. It's a real pleasure to meet you."

Cindi held out a hand. "Pleased to meet ya, honey."

Preston finally found his voice and wrapped his hand around her upper arm. He felt her wince and glanced down. "What the hell is that?"

"My new tattoo! Don't you just love it? I know how much you like to nibble and suck at the one on my boob, so I had them put a pink Tootsie Roll Pop on my arm." She pressed her fingertips against her lips. "Guess I shouldn't say that in mixed company."

He put his lips to her ear. Cheap perfume smacked him in the face. "What the hell are you doing?"

"Joining you for dinner, sweet cakes." She grinned and patted him on the cheek. "Let's sit down. I'm starving. Spent my lunch hour at the salon to get gussied up for tonight. You don't take me to nice places 'cause I'm no one special." No sooner had Cindi taken a seat than the waiter arrived.

"Would you like something to drink?" He managed to ask the question with a straight face.

"Oh, honey, I sure would. How about a strawberry daiquiri? The color will match my dress and tattoo. Could you please ask the bartender to add a couple extra cherries?" She winked at a gaping Preston and leaned in closer, offering a glimpse of her cleavage. "You didn't get my cherry, but I'll give you one from my drink."

Preston had never experienced the humiliation of being put on a hot seat and suffered the eyes of the other diners taking in the spectacle at their table, including his very good friend and boss. Lincoln was smiling and offered a thumbs-up!

"I'm so glad you could join us for dinner," Jen told her. "Preston said you work for the same company and are good friends."

"Oh, honey, we are *very* good friends. PJ is quite the stud. Sometimes I walk by his office and have to fan myself just thinking about his hot loving. But we can't tell anybody."

"PJ?"

"His name is Preston James, and calling him Preston is so formal. I call him PJ when we are humping like rabbits. He's goes like a real jackhammer."

Jen burst out laughing and took a good long drink of scotch. She really, really liked this woman.

Preston, too, reached for his glass and drank it down. When the waiter brought Cindi's drink with four cherries, he ordered another, a double. Nibble on her tit! Jackhammer! He wasn't a violent man, but right now he wanted to toss her over his shoulder and beat her bare naked bottom!

"I like your dress. I have one that is similar, but it's midnight-blue and not quite as sparkly." Jennie wondered what game Cindi was playing. She couldn't be for real. Could she? Her brother was beside himself with embarrassment. Good! He needed shaking up.

Cindi's eyes darted to the left, to the right, and then she lowered her voice to make sure they wouldn't be overheard. "It's on loan for the evening. The top is too big for my little boobs so I had to stuff it with socks. I borrowed the sparkly silver shoes from Jojo, my hairdresser and my feet are killing me. No one is supposed to know, but she's having an affair with the UPS guy. He's a real hottie, but not as spicy as my PJ."

She'd never thought of her brother as spicy, but it sounded good. "You have my sympathy." Jen smiled with understanding. "I'm not partial to high heels."

There was nothing wrong with Preston's hearing, and his eyes darted to the front of her dress. The heart-shaped neckline definitely enhanced the fullness of her breasts. Were they really small? Without those blasted ankle breakers, she was on the shorter side, but the clingy material evidenced she was all woman.

After the waiter took their dinner orders, Cindi decided to turn up the heat a little more. She pretended to drop her napkin and slid the strap off the back of her foot. "Sorry, I'm not used to fancy cloth. We have paper at my house." She lifted her foot, and felt for the bottom of his dress trousers and casually walked her toes up the front of his leg. When all he did was give her the evil eye, the stupid bell went off in her head. She was feeling up his prosthetic leg. Cindi never claimed to have a great sense of direction, but her second attempt hit pay dirt. Her toes walked up the inside of his upper leg to discover his warm crotch.

Preston sipped his second drink and wondered at the sultry challenge in her eyes. When the bottom of her foot settled in his groin, he forced himself to appear unmoved by her seductive action. He was tempted to reach under the tablecloth and grab her foot when she started to wiggle her toes. He gave her a venomous glare that said "stop." Now he'd have to sit through dinner with a damn hard-on!

"Hmm, isn't this juicy," Cindi said, wrapping her lips around one of the cherries. The bold challenge in her eyes never left his murderous stare. She took another cherry from her glass. "Here's the cherry I promised," she said and dangled it close to his lips. When he didn't immediately open his mouth, she pursed her lips in a pout. "No, you don't want my cherry."

The sexy move shot a hot message straight to his overheated groin. Damn, he was getting harder by the second. The longer he hesitated accepting her seductive invitation, the more attention they were drawing. He grabbed her wrist and bit the red temptation off at the stem.

Jennie looked at her brother and then at Cindi. They were playing a very sexy game, and she was tempted to pick up her napkin and fan herself. "Suddenly I feel like a third wheel. Would you two rather be alone?"

He totally ignored his sister's question and decided enough was enough. He didn't know what he had said or done to make Cindi play this game, but it was time to teach Ms. Cindi Pearl Sullivan a lesson. He slid his chair closer to her side of the table and casually walked his fingers up her arm, pausing to outline the lollipop tattoo. "Playtime is over. My turn," he whispered.

He turned to his sister. "Jen, I think it's only fair to tell you that before Cindi came to work for Adams Security, she had a somewhat carefree life, but she's mended her ways. I'm her one and only." Preston put a finger under her chin and turned her very tempting mouth in to his. He only wanted to feather her candy-pink lips, but he was lost the second he touched her mouth. Lips, oh so soft, molded to his. He forgot where they were and his purpose of teaching her a lesson. This was his Cindi, and he let himself enjoy.

He'd turned the tables on her, and Cindi didn't know how to react to his direct assault. Heat brushed the surface of her lips, stealing her breath. Should she move in, object or just enjoy. In the end, she thought *what the hell*, and let herself savor the feel of his wonderful mouth. It was a natural instinct to lower her hand beneath the tablecloth and seek out his crotch.

Jen cleared her throat. These two were hot and the other diners were getting an eyeful, including Lincoln Adams and his wife. "Excuse me. If you two can pull yourselves away from each other, the waiter would like to serve our dinner." This was the first real emotion she'd witnessed in her brother in years. Cindi challenged him as an undamaged man. Whatever this woman was doing, Jennie prayed it would be enough to bring him back to the person he was before he lost a part of himself.

"Sorry." Again, Preston didn't know what came over him. Cindi just—he didn't know—she made him react and do things like a normal man. It was wrong, totally wrong. For reasons no one would understand, he couldn't get involved with her or any woman. This evening would be the end of things between them. Treig Taylor could satisfy her needs. The thought resurrected the pain around his heart.

On the other side of the room, Jessie Taylor-Adams couldn't stand not knowing what was going on with Cindi and Preston.

"Why would they want to keep it a secret that they are dating?"

Lincoln signed the charge slip for their dinner and finished off the last of his coffee. "I'm as confused as you are. Even when we were in Manhattan, nothing was ever mentioned about him getting involved with a woman."

"Good, you're finished." Jessie stood up. "Come on, introduce me to his sister."

Lincoln grasped his wife's hand. "What are you up to, Lieutenant Adams?"

"I think I've been bitten by the Nose Patrol, busybodies who thrive on the gossip bug."

Cindi's heartbeat double-timed the closer her boss and his wife got to their table. They made such a beautiful couple. One would never suspect Jessie was pregnant in her slim-fitting white summer dress. Ideally, Lincoln would be tolerant of another "Cindi misadventure." This wasn't as bad as the time she kept Cupcake and Muffin in his Manhattan office for a week. The evening had gone downhill since she put her nail through that damn stocking—no, since her hair turned green! Escape was uppermost in her mind.

"Hope you enjoyed your dinner." Lincoln kept a possessive arm around his wife's waist and smiled at Preston's sister. "Jennie, we were about to leave, but I wanted you to meet my wife, Jessie."

Jen pushed away from the table and held out her hand. "The pleasure is mine. I can't get over how nice everyone has been. They've made me feel a part of the community, and I haven't even gotten the job."

Jessie raised a brow at the god-awful color of Cindi's hair before shifting her stare to Preston. "You two certainly know how to keep a secret. That was quite a show you put on the other night at my promotion party, pretending not to like each other. I don't know why you've wanted to keep your relationship quiet. As far as I know, Lincoln doesn't have a policy stating coworkers can't date."

"I was also surprised. Preston never mentioned he was seriously involved." Jennie gave her brother a pointed stare. "Cindi Pearl is perfect for him."

Leave it to his sister to add coal to the fire. Preston silently mouthed, "*I'll get you for that.*"

"It's a shame you have to leave tomorrow. You'll be missing a great weekend," Jessie added. "Our Fourth of July celebration got rained out two weeks ago and has been rescheduled for tomorrow. The parade is at noon, followed by games in the park and a chicken-and-ribs barbeque in the afternoon, hosted by our volunteer fire department and first aid squad. Live music starts at six, followed by fireworks as soon as it gets dark. It would be a good time for you to mingle with the citizens." Jessie decided not to elaborate on the special service they were having for their newly erected veteran's memorial. The object was to make sure Preston was in the audience.

"I haven't been to a small town celebration in…" Jennie paused. "No, I've never been. You've convinced me to stay until Monday. It will also be the perfect opportunity to spend more time with Cindi Pearl."

Preston inwardly blanched at her announcement. He produced an unenthusiastic smile. "Oh, goodie."

"You'll have a great time." Jessie put a hand to her stomach. "Cindi, I feel a little queasy and need to make a stop in the ladies' room. I could use the company."

Lincoln's complexion paled, and he put a hand to his wife's arm. "Are you sick? Do you want me to come with you?"

She lifted a brow and patted his very handsome face. "Unless society has gone off the deep end and changed the rules, men aren't allowed in the ladies' room. Talk to Preston and tell Jennie she's got the job."

Cindi stood up, forgetting she was shoeless on one foot. Hotness swept her cheeks when she reached under the table and retrieved her shoe. She couldn't resist one more teasing dig. "Sorry, I discovered something very hot and hard under my foot." Cindi turned about and limped off, dangling her shoe from the tip of her finger.

"She is quite a woman," Jennie laughed. "Now, about that job."

"What the hell is going on?" Jessie demanded the moment they stepped into the ladies' room. Luckily the three stalls were empty.

Cindi plopped down in a dainty white metal chair and took off her other shoe. "My feet are killing me! Do you have to throw up or something?"

"No, it was just a ploy to get you alone." Jessie brushed a finger down one of the wide green stripes in Cindi Pearl's hair. "Did you do this on purpose?"

"It was supposed to be pink, but my home color project failed miserably." Cindi plucked at the tight fabric that molded her hips. "As for why I'm dressed like a hooker…" Cindi explained about Preston helping her out with the derby accounting problem and pretending to be his un-girlfriend.

"Remind me to kick him in his ass for saying you were no one special."

"Thanks, Jessie. I needed that," Cindi said with a half smile.

"Lincoln told me about the sick gift. I'd like to strangle the person myself. I wrote up a report about the theft, just to keep everything legal. I'll sit on it until I hear different from my husband." Jessie tucked a finger under the shoulder strap of Cindi's dress and tugged it up. "For a minute I thought you had a boob job on your lunch hour. One of your Adidases was showing."

"Thanks. A do-it-yourself sock job is a lot cheaper. I'll be glad when this night is over."

"How do you think Preston is going to react to our ceremony tomorrow night? I purposely invited his sister as a way to make sure he shows up. I also think it's time she met the real Cindi Pearl. You can't continue your ditzy blonde routine the rest of the weekend. As the saying goes, the truth will set you free."

"That is great advice. I once heard Lincoln describe a situation as a cluster-fuck. I believe I am experiencing one firsthand."

CHAPTER 5

The following morning, Cindi literally rolled out of bed. She'd only had one drink, but her body felt like she'd downed Jell-O shots all night. Her feet still hurt, and a blister had formed on the bottom of her big toe. After taking a ten-minute shower and washing her hair three times, she studied the hangdog face in the oval mirror over the bathroom sink and winced. The directions on the box of "Quick Highlights" promised the temporary color would wash out. Unfortunately, puke-green streaks still blended with her blond hair. She hoped the stain wouldn't be so obvious when her hair dried. If she was thinking clearly, she'd call Preston and tell him to stuff his invitation, but that would be disappointing Jen, whom Cindi really liked. The disastrous evening was her own doing, so she'd have to grin and bear the consequences.

It was too early to get ready for her so-called "date" to show Jennie around the town, so she didn't bother with underwear and stepped into her old denim cutoffs and pulled on a lacy white camisole. She grabbed her silk robe from the back of the bathroom door before going downstairs. While living in Manhattan, she'd found the kimono in a secondhand shop in Chinatown, and she'd always wondered what the Chinese lettering between the red hibiscus flowers meant.

The new-day sun penetrated the three valance-draped windows that faced the eastern sky, brightening the country kitchen, which was decorated in a soft blue. Sam had left a note on the kitchen table. *What happened last night, hubba-hubba?* Cindi shook her head. Her best friend didn't know the half of it. The temperature on the big round thermometer on the metal garden shed close to the house read seventy-five degrees, and it was only eight o'clock. It was going to be a hot one. She opted for a tall glass of iced sun tea and drank it down on her way to the adjoining mud room to get her cowgirl boots and the straw hat she wore doing farm chores.

The lower section of the stone-and-frame barn was much cooler and smelled of fresh hay. Cream Puff had left four eggs and was on the perching rod over the wood- frame nesting box. Cookie paced like an expectant father, undoubtedly wondering what was keeping breakfast. Roosters were known to announce the day as soon as the sun came up, but this farm's proud fowl cock-a-doodled whenever the mood struck. He'd recently started wearing a doll-sized top hat, thanks to Edith Amanda.

"Thank you, guys, for the eggs." Cindi changed the straw in the nesting box and the ducks' beds, not that they ever used them. The free-spirited sisters nested any place their little duck hearts desired. More times than not, they could be found among the tall reeds, tiger lilies and cattails that rimmed the freshwater pond in the rear of property. She mucked out the cow and calf's space and gave all the critters food and water.

The hot, humid air slicked her skin the moment she stepped outside, and she pushed the straw hat off her forehead. Time for another shower, she decided. Her next stop was the thriving vegetable garden alongside the equipment shed. The beefsteak tomatoes had reddened enough to be picked. A couple had fallen to the ground and started to soften, so she added them to her basket.

The sound of a car coming down the drive drew her attention. She walked around the side of the stone house and stopped short at the sight of Preston Reynolds exiting his dark copper Aston Martin convertible. He certainly wasn't shy driving a three-hundred-thousand-dollar car. What else did he have to spend his money on? Certainly not women. She was surprised he owned a pair of designer jeans and a T-shirt. The edge of the cloud-white sleeves gripped the pronounced muscles on the upper part of his arms, and the tightened material across his chest emphasized his firm rib cage. His tight-ass personality appeared to be firmly in place, and his mirrored sunglasses couldn't mask his angry scowl. He looked good enough to eat, and she wouldn't have minded sinking her teeth into his abs.

Preston had never been angrier in his life and decided to have it out with Cindi Pearl. He needed to set some ground rules so they could get through the rest of the weekend without a repeat of the previous evening, but his tongue was glued to the roof of his mouth. She was the sexiest hillbilly he'd ever seen, sauntering toward him in cowgirl boots, swinging a wicker basket. The slight breeze spread the opening of the flowery kimono that flirted with the bottom of her very brief denim shorts. A major hard-on sprang to life when her thin camisole revealed the shadow of dark nipples and pointed breasts. He swallowed hard. No, they were not small. A stronger breeze caught the brim of her hat and whipped it off her head. When she bent over to pick it up, the denim rode high on her delicious butt cheeks, and it was evident she wasn't wearing underwear. He groaned inwardly. This time he couldn't accuse her of trying to entice or seduce him, because she'd had no knowledge he was coming to see her.

She took a bold stance and immediately went on the offensive. "What the hell do you want? How do you know where I live?"

"I work for the same security company, remember? Why did you pull that crazy-ass stunt last night? You looked and acted like a Times Square hooker! I've never been so embarrassed in my life!"

"I'm surprised you even know where to find one! I overheard you telling your sister that I wasn't anyone special, just a nice woman you work with and give an occasional poke. You have some nerve! You hurt my feelings!" Cindi jabbed him in the chest with her pointer finger, forgetting her sharp nail extensions. "You know what's wrong with you?"

"No, but I'm sure you're about to tell me," he sneered.

"You are so out-to-lunch with your damn figures and computers. You're too serious, too stringent, too proper. Your face would probably crack if you smiled! In other words, you're a tight-ass son of a bitch who doesn't give a damn about anyone but himself."

Preston stiffened at her insults. "You have some nerve tossing offensive adjectives at me."

"Listen to yourself! You don't even know how to insult me without using proper English."

"You want proper insults, Ms. Sullivan?" He leaned in to her face. Their noses were almost touching. "How's this? You are as graceless as a ballerina with two left feet. If they put a small hole in the middle of a football field, your clumsy, inept self would step in it! The Band-Aid manufacturers reference you every time they give profit reports to their stockholders!"

"Hah! I'll give you clumsy. How's this?" Cindy backed away and reached into her overflowing basket for a soft tomato. She brought her arm back like a baseball pitcher on a mound and aimed for his head. His reflexes were better than she expected, and he dodged the red projectile. Unfortunately, it splattered against the windshield of his three-hundred-thousand-dollar car. "Whoops!" she giggled and took off like a bat out of hell toward the barn. Breathless, she ran up the concrete ramp to the main level, and all thoughts of escape died away. The huge doors were slightly ajar, and the iron bar, which usually bolted the double doors to keep out unwanted predators and curious animals, dangled from iron support bolts. They never forgot to set the bolt. She didn't turn at the sound of Preston's hurried footsteps coming up the ramp.

"You little..." He stopped. All the playfulness was gone from her paled features. "What is it?"

"We never leave this open." Cindi noticed he wasn't even breathing heavily from his jaunt after her.

"Maybe Samantha just forgot?"

"No, we learned our lesson the hard way. A few months back we got three chickens, and a fox literally got into the hen house. We've since moved Cookie and Cream Puff to the lower level and raised their nesting boxes."

Preston raised a brow. "Cookie? Cream Puff?"

"Our rooster and hen. We also have a cow named Pound Cake and Brownie, her calf. We named them after sweet treats since Sam is going to open a tea shop and bakery."

"Makes sense. Come on, let's take a look inside. Let me go first."

The smell hit them the moment they stepped into the huge open space. "I'll turn on the overhead lights." Cindi put a hand over her mouth because of the foul odor, but also the surprise that occupied the center of the room. Someone had gifted them a huge mound of black plastic bags. They'd been split open to allow rotten-smelling garbage to escape.

Preston pushed his sunglasses to the top of his head. "Why would someone dump this shit in here?"

"All that fresh garbage would attract predators. See those steps on the side of the room? They go to the lower level, where we keep our livestock. I think this was meant to be my second warning."

"What are you talking about, second warning?"

Cindi wiped the sweat from her brow with the sleeve of her kimono and told him about the critter with the broken neck, Jessie filing a private police report and Lincoln covering their derby expenses so the kids wouldn't be disappointed.

"Your request to find the missing money just became a top priority." Preston glanced around the cool interior. "This doesn't look like an ordinary barn. Everything appears to have been updated. The wood walls are refinished. The black iron drop lighting is unique. You could have a barn dance in here. Where does that set of steps lead?"

"Come on. I'll show you."

Preston followed her up the iron stairway, but his eyes had found a permanent home on her cute butt that swayed enticingly with each step she took. This couldn't and shouldn't be happening. His visit was supposed to be short and sweet. He'd meant to tell her to ditch the ditzy blonde routine and be herself for the rest of the weekend, but he was so caught up in his own heightening hard-on, he almost missed her explanation.

"The previous owner's wife was an artist and needed her own space, so he finished off the loft area. This is where she did her work." Cindi's soft voice echoed throughout the open space, which included six rectangular skylights and sun-brightened windows. "Samantha found a few paintings and contacted the late artist's husband. He said the apartment had a very special meaning. They called it their love nest." Cindi led him down a short hall and stepped into a bedroom with a high vaulted ceiling. "As you can see, he left the bed frame and mattress."

"Is that a sample of her work?" Preston asked. Two white doves, their wings spread wide in flight, holding a red heart, had been painted on the wall behind the bed. The artist's fine hand had written, *You are my life, my happiness, my love.*

"She did beautiful work. The birds appear so real, you want to reach out and touch them."

"Through there is a full, designer bathroom. He had it equipped with everything she needed, including an intercom directly into the house."

"He was certainly being overprotective."

"Oh, his wife was in a car accident when she was in her late thirties and lost an arm and the use of one leg. He had a special chair lift installed, but Sam had it removed."

When her narration was met with heavy silence, Cindi spun about. The quietness in the room pressed against her ears, but it was the hungry look on his face that heightened her senses. She put a hand to her throat and tried to make light of the situation. "Tour's over. Time to go downstairs and clean up the mess."

The next thing she knew, her hat went flying across the room, and his hands found her shoulders. "Preston?" she choked out.

"You are driving me freaking crazy!" He slowly guided her backward to the edge of the bare mattress. "Even when you are being sweet Cindi Pearl and not that blonde dingbat, all I want to do is taste that mouth." They landed on the soft bed with him on top. "Don't move. I need to get this out of my system. If you don't want me to kiss you, tell me now."

Cindi didn't know what was going to happen and didn't care. Preston's solid form had her pinned to the bed, and she wanted him. She wanted it all, but a kiss was a very nice place to start.

When she remained silent, he got his answer. He wanted to devour her mouth in one quick kiss and get her out of his system, but this might be his only time to enjoy her. He lowered his head and stroked the surface of her lips with his own, savoring her sweet, honey-like softness. The luscious taste of her shattered his self-control, and he shivered with hot desire. *Caution be damned*, he thought and relished every facet of her tantalizing body. He was lost.

This was the kiss of her dreams, from the man of her dreams, so she let herself take pleasure in his manly scent, his strong body and his steel hardness that found a warm resting place between her thighs. Their heartbeats joined, beating out of control. She wanted to run her fingertips down his back, memorize the feel of his muscles, experience his heat, but he told her not to move.

She was more than he desired. When he raised his head, his eyes fell on her kiss-swollen lips. One taste and he'd become addicted. She opened her mouth to say something, but he silenced her with a finger. "More?" he whispered. At her slight nod, he threw caution to the wind and delighted in her mouth one last time.

He reluctantly ended the kiss and brushed a few greenish hairs off her forehead. The sun had pinked her cheeks and the tip of her nose. "You know this can't go any further. I can't make love to you."

"*Bullshit*," Cindi wanted to scream. The proof of his arousal pressing against her confirmed there was nothing wrong with the male mechanics of his body. She wouldn't push, but called his bluff. "Can't or won't?"

"Can't. I like you Cindi, really like you, but there are limitations to what I can offer a woman."

"I've never been a greedy person, so I'll take whatever I can get." *For now.*

Temptation drew him to sample her lips one more time, but something jumped on his back, and a soft furry body planted itself between his shoulder blades. He turned his head and encountered a wet nose. "And who is this?"

"Meet the real Donut," Cindi laughed, tickling the pygmy goat under his chin.

"Be careful when you get up. Our two ducks, Cupcake and Muffin, are probably right behind. The three are practically inseparable. I call them the three amigos."

"How do I get him off my neck?"

Cindi scooped up the pygmy goat by the belly. "Come here, you rascal. Let the man up."

When they went downstairs, Cupcake and Muffin were squatting on the plastic bags, and their incessant quacking echoed throughout the high-ceilinged barn. "Yes, I know this garbage shouldn't be here," Cindi soothed. "I'll let Jessie know what we found and then tackle this mess."

"Let's take some pictures first. Maybe we'll find something with a personal address to indicate where this crap came from. I'll give you a hand and then go home and take a shower. I have to pick up Jennie at eleven-thirty. Are you going to be all right here alone?"

"I'll be fine. These animals are my protectors." When they had more time, she'd tell him about the ducks playing hero and helping capture a killer.

After they notified Jessie of their find and bagged the garbage, Cindi walked Preston to his car. "Don't pick me up. I'll park in the rear of the Spoonful and meet you in front of Jack's Pizzeria."

He paused before opening the driver's side door. "I have two questions. Who is going to join me for the rest of the weekend? Cindi Pearl or your alter ego?"

"Me," she laughed. "Question two?"

"Is there anything between you and TJ?"

Cindi sensed a bit of jealousy in his question. "Do you mean is Treig John Taylor my significant other?"

"Yes."

"No. We dated for a while and remain good friends, hang-out buddies of sorts."

He couldn't resist and put a hand to the back of her neck. "Good." What followed was a long, sweet kiss.

"Yes!" Cindi watched him back out of the driveway and danced all the way into the house.

CHAPTER 6

The town of Laurel Heights might have been a small, rural community, but the citizens knew how to hold a celebration. Spectators jockeyed for position on the sidewalk to view the parade, waving American flags and holding colorful balloons. The new light poles that lined Main Street were draped in red, white and blue swags. Members of the police and fire departments, holding American and state flags, led the parade, followed by Mayor Margaret Taylor, the Grand Marshal. Dressed in a white suit with a red carnation pinned to the collar of her fitted jacket, she perched on the backseat of a white Cadillac convertible and waved to the crowd. High school and middle school bands followed, along with the first aid units and the volunteer fire department. Boy Scout and Girl Scout troops added to the colorful assortment of hometown marchers.

A newly formed group of elementary school children, dressed up like a fife and drum corps, escorted a bright red farm tractor that pulled an open-sided wagon of senior citizens decked out in patriotic colors. Motorcycles, bicycles and tricycles sporting crepe paper–decorated wheels rode honor guard along the parade path.

"This is fantastic!" Jen bubbled with excitement, waving a flag in one hand and holding a star-shaped helium balloon in the other. "Oh my God, look at those women. Standing together, their sack dresses resemble the American flag."

"That's the infamous ladies' bridge club," Cindi said. A loud clanging bell drew everyone's attention to the flatbed truck supporting a replica of the old Baldwin train manned by Northrup Whipper. "I don't know of any other occasion where a person wants to march in a parade," she told Jen. "Even you are wearing red, white and blue."

"All I had was that ugly suit, a pair of shorts, a tank top and jeans. The clerk in the Last Chance Motel told me about the new boutique that opened in the train station across from the Adams Security building. I had Preston make a quick stop before we came to the parade. The white capris and blue-and-white tank were marked down." Jennie wiggled her foot. "Even these adorable red sandals were on sale."

"My sundress came from the same shop. I'm glad it came with the white bolero jacket or my shoulders would be as red as my dress. With the shop so close, sometimes I run over there on my lunch hour." Cindi tipped her head to the side. "I don't normally wear wide-brimmed hats, but not all of the green streaks washed out of my hair."

"I was quite impressed by the beautiful new building and those condos by the depot. If my plans work out, I'll need a place to live." Jennie suddenly realized the folding chair next to Cindi was empty. "Where did Preston go?"

"He spotted Lincoln near the grandstand and wanted to talk to him about something important. Since our boss is now on the town council, he has to mingle with the rest of the politicians."

"I'm glad Preston isn't here so we can talk. Last night, I saw right through your wonderful performance. You are exactly what he needs to drag him out of his stiff, introverted shell." Jennie took in a deep breath and needed an answer to a question that had been bugging her since last evening. "Are you really an item?"

The words Jessie had said last evening popped into Cindi's head: *the truth will set you free.* "Yes and no. He asked me to dinner as a front to convince you he wasn't gay and was still interested in women. I wanted to teach him a lesson."

Jennie's green eyes widened. "I only said that as a joke! Growing up, he had a problem keeping his zipper up! Cindi, I can read my brother like a book. Dolphin avoids relationships and intimacy because he fears a woman will look at him like he's a freak."

"Dolphin? That's a name I've never heard."

"That was his nickname growing up because he loved to surf. He spent so much time in the water, my parents were worried he would grow a dorsal fin."

"I can't imagine a woman thinking a loved one a freak. I don't treat him like a person who wears a prosthetic leg and have tried to make him understand he is a normal man. Of course, there are limitations and expectations. Unfortunately, I've gone about proving my point ass-backward. Preston is very special to me." Cindi looked away and watched the next float. Mrs. Clark sat at the head of a friendship circle made up of the ladies from the Trinity Church Needler's Club. All had donned white wigs and colonial dresses. Spread across their laps was a crocheted flag of the original thirteen American colonies.

"I think it is a little more than that," Jennie challenged when the float had passed. "Only love would drive you to extremes, like last night."

"You're a mind reader, too," Cindi laughed softly. "Between us, I love him, but he doesn't love himself. I've got a plan that I pray will help him realize life is worth living. Please don't ask me any details, because they aren't final."

"Whatever you are doing seems to be working. When he picked me up earlier, he was—I don't know—laid back, like a guy who just got his rocks off. I was also surprised to see he's into the theme of things and wore a Western-cut short-sleeve shirt in red, white and blue. When he reaches for your hand, I don't think he's using it for support."

Despite the heat, Cindi hoped the heightened color to her cheeks wasn't obvious. "This morning he came to see me. After we tossed insults at each other, he zapped my world with the kind of kisses a woman only dreams about."

"Hot damn!" Jennie grinned. "Sounds like your plan is working." She reached into her canvas carryall and passed Cindi a card with her personal cell phone number and e-mail address. "Please keep in touch. I'm very interested in my brother's well-being and progress, if you get my drift."

"In other words, you want to know when he takes off like a jackhammer."

"Close enough." Jennie's smile clouded over. "I have a small favor."

"Sure."

"Before I leave Monday morning, I would love to hear him laugh. You would never know it, but he has a hearty laugh and a beautiful smile. Here he comes. Mum's the word."

"I'll see what I can do."

Preston headed back to Cindi and his sister, reflecting on his conversation with Lincoln, which covered setting up additional security on the soap box derby accounts and filling him in on the garbage incident in the barn. When Cindi had related the episode about the mangled critter, he felt hurt that she hadn't brought him into her confidence right away. Lincoln agreed to go along with Preston's conspiracy to be in a better position if there was additional trouble on the farm. He couldn't give her what she needed physically, but he could protect the woman who occupied a special place in his heart from potential harm. Considering the way she had responded to his kisses that morning, he wondered if his feelings were just one-sided. He was sinking deeper and deeper into a quicksand of desire and had no idea how he was going to survive. The initial pain he'd suffered losing his leg was mild compared to the anguish he'd experience when it was time to walk away from Cindi. He couldn't think about that now and decided to enjoy every precious moment with her.

"How's the parade going?" he asked, taking his seat beside Cindi. In a natural move, he reached for her hand, linked their fingers and brushed his lips on the corner of her brow.

She loved that he immediately felt the need to touch her. And the butterfly kiss, in public? *Don't start psychoanalyzing his tenderness.* "You missed Mrs. Schmidt and the bridge ladies dressed up like the American flag."

"Ah, one of the seven wonders of the world."

"You made a joke," Jennie chided with a laugh. "Will wonders never cease?"

"Didn't I just say something like that, *Jennifer?*" he countered.

"You are such a smartass, *Preston James.*"

"And your point would be?"

"Children, behave, or I won't buy you popcorn when we watch the fireworks," Cindy teased before turning to Preston. "Were you able to speak with Lincoln?"

"Yes. I filled him in on what happened this morning. He plans to upgrade the exterior security on the farm to include all the outbuildings. Monday I start my investigation in earnest." He gave her hand a loving squeeze.

As soon as the parade ended, the onlookers mingled with the marchers. They were just about to head for the Spoonful when Edie Adams came running up, followed by her parents. Jessie's new lieutenant bars glinted on the collar of her white uniform shirt.

"Cindi, did you see me!" Edie's voice sparkled with excitement and she spun around, making her long black braids fly like a kite. "Bet you can't guess who I represent, dressed in this old Girl Scout uniform?"

"Let me see." Cindi tapped her lips, watching the impatience build up on the face of the ten-year-old dressed in the unadorned olive-green linen dress that almost brushed the tops of her favorite high-top sneakers.

"Juliette Gordon Low!" Edith blurted. "She founded the Girl Scouts in 1912 and was practically deaf, but that didn't stop her. Are you coming to the games in the park? They are going to have a pie eating contest, sack races and everything! Daddy is going to be my partner. He even ordered a real cotton candy–making machine because Mommy loves cotton candy." Edie didn't stop to take a breath and looked at Preston. "Mr. Reynolds, you should run with Cindi in the sack race!"

The word *limitations* flashed through Cindi's mind, and she quickly offered an excuse. "Maybe next time. I'm wearing a new dress and, knowing how clumsy I can be, I'd probably fall and get it full of grass stains." No one other than Cindi was aware of the fingers that gripped her hand in gratitude.

Jen was enchanted by the young girl. "Hi, Edie. I'm Jennie, Mr. Reynolds's sister. I recognized you right away. Did you know that Juliette's middle name was Daisy and they named the first level of Girl Scouting after Ms. Low?"

Edie held out her hand. "Yes. I researched her for my school project. You're the lady who is going to run the community center. It's named after my grandfather, Norman Taylor."

Before coming east, Jennie had researched the town's history. Norman Taylor was a prominent attorney and judge. "He was a wonderful man. Will you be taking any of the dance or gymnastics classes that will be offered?"

"You are asking the wrong questions," Jessie said, putting her hands on Edie's shoulders. "Her favorite sports are soccer, basketball and fishing." Jessie's radio went off. "Sorry, duty calls. Kids are trying to set the woods on fire with illegal fireworks. See you all later," she said and hurried across the street.

"Isn't she going to have a baby?" Jennie asked Lincoln.

"Yes, but there's no stopping her for now. Can I interest anyone in lunch at the Spoonful, my treat?

Jennie was further impressed by the camaraderie of the townsfolk competing against each other in games. They cheered on Edie and Lincoln in the sack race, along with their close friends, Lisa Kay and Sam Morlock, her fiancé, who was also a member of the town council. The volunteer firemen had set up a dunking booth, with all proceeds going to their annual fund-raising campaign. No one seemed to mind getting wet since the temperature pushed to ninety degrees. The games had almost concluded when Sallie Mae approached Cindi and Preston in a panic.

"Just who I need! We lost two judges in the pie eating contest, and you two just volunteered."

The owner of the Spoonful personified the colors in the American flag, right down the small flag sticking out of her white straw hat. Cindi shrugged a shoulder and looked at Preston. "I'm game if you are."

"Sure, why not?"

"Can I enter the contest?" Jennie asked.

"The more the merrier," Sallie Mae laughed. "Come with me to the table next to the gazebo and sign up."

With hands clasped, Cindi and Preston enjoyed the special closeness they'd established that morning and strolled down the brick-lined path toward the contest staging area. Red geraniums and white petunias thrived in the tall urns that flanked the park benches. Two other judges, members of the town council, were standing in front of two long tables covered with green plastic tarps. Blueberry pies, topped with hills of whipped cream, had been placed before each of the fifteen contestants. The committee had provided clear plastic ponchos for contestants and judges to protect their clothes. Jennie had claimed a spot next to Lincoln and Jessie.

"I hope my sister realizes no hands are allowed."

"Why do you think I didn't volunteer?"

A devilish gleam filled Preston's eyes as he studied the mounds of fluffy cream covering the pies. "I don't know. You would look cute with a nose full of whipped cream."

"Don't even think about it!" Cindi backed away and adjusted the thin poncho to make sure her entire dress was covered. "Get ready, smart guy. As soon as Sallie Mae toots the air horn, start walking around the table to make sure no one uses hands or whips out a spoon."

The loud horn blasted the air, and the eating frenzy began. The surrounding crowd cheered on the pie eaters. It took all of two minutes for the winner to demolish his pie, including the crust. Preston was lucky enough to be behind the young boy and shot his arm in the air.

"We have the winner!" he announced. A string of laughing blue faces congratulated Kyle, the chief of police's twelve-year-old grandson.

"Well, how was it?" Preston asked, watching his sister clean her face with napkins and wet wipes. Lincoln and Jessie concentrated on cleaning each other's faces and sneaking in little kisses.

"Fantastic. I only took a couple of bites because I couldn't stop laughing. It was delicious, but a lot messier than I anticipated."

"Better you than me," Preston sneered.

"Oh, really?" The devil invaded her body and she decided to have a bit more fun. "Remember how much we shared growing up? No time like the present." Jennie picked up what was left of her pie and let it fly directly at her brother.

Once again, his reflexes saved him from getting sacked by the blue projectile. Unfortunately, the pie connected with Cindi Pearl's face.

"Oh my God! I am so sorry," Jennie cried in horror, coming around the table with the entire package of wipes.

Preston's lips tightened at the comical sight and swiped a finger across the pointed peak of cream on Cindi's nose. He popped the sample in his mouth. "Hmm, delicious." He winked.

"Since you like it so much..." Cindi picked up Jessie's partially eaten pie and smashed it in Preston's handsome face. "Have the whole damn pie!"

"Right on!" Jennie laughed and held up her hand to give Cindi a high five.

Once again their adolescent behavior drew attention, and everyone laughed at their matching purplish-blue-and-white faces. The pie filling slid down their cheeks and dripped off their jaws, and globs landed on the plastic protecting their clothes. Their noses resembled snow-covered Mt. Everest.

"How do you like it?" Cindi spewed. "Not so fast ducking this time!"

Preston was trying to get a handle on what just happened. Something opened inside, something that had been closed up tight for a long time. He burst out laughing, a hard, rollicking laugh. "Oh, Cindi Pearl, only you." He put his hands on her slime-covered shoulders, drew her in and kissed her—goop, whipped cream and all.

The spectators started clapping.

Only one person noticed the tears running down Jennie Reynolds's face. She turned to face a smiling Lincoln Adams.

"I think he'll begin to heal," Lincoln said.

All Jennie could do was nod.

The ladies from the Trinity Church auxiliary had provided mouth-watering desserts to go along with the evening barbecue, funded by the town, followed by live music and dancing. As soon as the sun dipped behind the trees, Margaret Taylor stepped up to the microphone on the stage of the gazebo and called everyone's attention.

"I hope you all enjoyed our July Fourth celebration." Margaret paused when a rousing cheer followed her statement. She turned toward the newly erected monument draped in a canvas sheath. "Everyone has been anxious to see our new war memorial, but we waited until today to hold our special ceremony."

All eyes shifted to the large video screen that had been placed to the side of the stage. Thanks to Lincoln Adams's clever e-team, a video had been put together combining patriotic music and pictures of fighting men, all the way back to the Civil War. At a nod from Margaret, the screen was filled with the US Naval Academy Glee Club singing "Eternal Father, strong to save…"

"The monument is to honor those who have died so that we enjoy our freedom," Margaret began. "The first person I would like to introduce is Northrup Whipper, honoring his relatives who fought in the Civil War. We are all one country, but his son Steven is representing the brave men who fought in the Confederate States Army."

Northrup walked proudly on the flagstone path to the monument, wearing the blue uniform of the Union Army along side his son, dressed in a gray uniform of the army of the South.

Pictures began to flash on the screen and the music changed to the "Marines' Hymn." *From the halls of Montezuma, to the shores of Tripoli…*

"Chuck McCarthy is representing his father and uncles who fought in World War II and Korea. The marine uniform belonged to his uncle. The naval officer in the photo he is carrying is his great-grandfather, who lost his life in World War I.

The video and music segued to the theme song of the US Air Force: *Off we go into the wild blue yonder…*"

"Representing the Vietnam War is Mr. Berweiler. As you can see, he served in the United States Air Force."

Lee Greenwood's voice rang out: *I'm proud to be an American.*

"Please welcome Captain Danielle Whipper," Margaret continued. "She flew a helicopter in Desert Storm."

He'd been set up. As the mayor introduced the veterans who represented wars and police actions, Preston's anger increased. He'd never bargained for this. The day had been perfect, right down to the pie fight. The laugh that had burst out was like a plug had come unsealed from his suppressed sense of humor. And the kiss he'd shared with Cindi was sweet and loving, despite the slimy blueberries and whipped cream. Now he sat on a folding chair among family and friends, telling himself this was not about to happen. He wasn't a hero. His fisted hands tightened and he lowered his eyes, unable to watch the pictures of uniformed comrades in the desert from hell.

Cindi sensed the tension radiating from Preston's body. They'd been holding hands, but when the pictures of soldiers in Iraq appeared, he withdrew his arm and hand. She'd known all along about the ceremony, but hadn't warned him. It was much too late to question if they'd done the right thing.

"And now to the present." Margaret inhaled deeply. "They aren't in uniform, but live among us, never bragging about their heroism and how they survived the horrors of war. I would ask everyone to stand up and recognize Lincoln Adams and Preston Reynolds. They have been chosen to unveil our memorial." Everyone started clapping, and the voice of the late Kate Smith singing "God Bless America" rang out from the speakers.

Every bone in Preston's body froze, but a gentle hand squeezed his arm. He turned his head, and the tears running down Cindi Pearl's face pierced his cold heart.

"You can do this—not just for yourself, but for all of the men and women who served alongside you. Honor their memory."

When a stronger, larger hand settled on his shoulder, he met Lincoln's gaze. "Come on. Don't make me go up there alone. Cindi is right. It's not just for us, but all of our buddies who never made it home."

The crowd—no —the entire town was waiting. He gave a quick nod and reluctantly stood up.

The veterans stood proudly at attention as the former Army Rangers walked side by side and approached the monument hemmed by a half circle of fluttering flags. Lincoln and Preston pulled on the white canvas, unveiling a rectangular marble stone in gleaming black. A ring of low spotlights highlighted the engraved spear that bore an American eagle supported by crossed flags. Names of fallen heroes had been etched in perfect alignment like soldiers at attention. There were very few dry eyes in the audience when "The Star-Spangled Banner" filled the night sky.

Lincoln's heart was filled with pride. He turned to his friend, who had saved his life and their patrol. "We have a lot to be thankful for."

Pain, hurt, anger spread through Preston's body like an out-of-control wildfire. Years of bitterness spilled out. "How can you say that? You wear an eye patch, and I lost a part of my goddamn leg."

Lincoln wasn't surprised by his buddy's outburst. It was a long time coming, but Linc understood what his friend was feeling. He clamped a hand on Preston's stiff shoulder.

"No, man, you don't get it. We are alive. Our names aren't up there."

Our names aren't up there, our names aren't up there repeated over and over in Preston's head, and he hoped to God the tears welling up in eyes weren't obvious. He almost choked on his next statement. "Linc, I don't know what to say." He had to get out of there before he made a fool of himself. "Do me a favor. Take Jennie back to the motel. Tell her I'll pick her up at ten and we'll go to breakfast at the Spoonful."

"What about Cindi?"

Preston's mind went momentarily blank. "What about Cindi?"

"Should I tell her you'll pick her up too?"

Panic began to set in. "Tell her I'll give her a call. I have to get out of here."

From across the lawn, Cindi and Jennie, choked up with emotion, stared at Preston and Lincoln. "I'd love to know what they are talking about," Jen said, brushing the tears from her cheeks. "Did you know they were going to do this tonight?"

"Yes." Tightness gripped Cindi's throat, and she could barely get the word out.

"Some people might think tossing him from the frying pan into the fire was being heartless and cruel," Jen said, "but he needed this wake-up jolt. The patriotic ceremony was beautifully done."

"Lincoln was part of the planning committee, so he knew what was going to happen. His staff compiled the video. If there was anything that might have been too graphic or upsetting, he would have had them edit it out."

"I wish our parents had been here to witness his heroism being recognized. I took a video of the ceremony and pictures of Lincoln and Preston removing the drape. I'll wait till tomorrow before I get a closer look at the memorial. There are too many people up there."

"You'll be able to share the pictures with your folks." Cindi wished she was standing next to Preston to give him her support.

The surrounding crowd was overwhelming and escape became impossible.

Citizens approached Preston and Lincoln and all the service men and offered their hands, repeating the same phrase: "Thank you for your service."

When Jessie stepped up to Lincoln, suggesting they start heading over to the lake for the fireworks, Preston saw the opportunity to make his escape. He never looked back and hurried down the walking path through the deserted section of the park. Fingers of moonlight illuminated the paved path, and the leaf-heavy trees and thick ground foliage made it the perfect place to seek solace. Sweat covered his brow, and the chicken and ribs he'd eaten at dinner was like a rock in his gut. Nausea roiled up and he barely made it to a garbage can and heaved, emptying his stomach. He felt spent and wiped out. The sick feeling was gone, but a mix of emotions lay heavy on his heart. He sat on a small patch of grass, buried his face in his hands and let the storm of tears fall.

Our names aren't up there repeated in his head.

"What happened?" Jessie asked when everyone finished shaking hands. "Preston was here a moment ago and just took off."

Lincoln drew his wife to the rear of the monument, which offered a small amount of privacy. "Remember what I said about him starting to heal? Well, I think tonight's ceremony was an emotional eye-opener. He's never accepted that he saved five guys from getting blown up, resulting in the loss of his lower right leg. Physically, he's learned to live with wearing a prosthetic leg and acts perfectly normal. It's the emotional scars banded around his heart that have kept him in a private hell. He is very much aware of the special program I established for the veterans on staff. Attending is optional. I've encouraged him to talk to one of the psychologists, but his standard answer is, 'I'm fine.' Cindi, in her own special way, has challenged his denial in letting himself enjoy a relationship with a woman."

Jessie brought her arms around his waist. "I know we've never really talked about your injury, but did you go through the same personal torment?"

Lincoln drew her closer, not caring that members of the Nose Patrol, the name he'd given the nosy bodies who thrived on gossip, were probably watching their every move. "When I got shot and was told I would lose the use of my eye, I went through a private hell the likes of which I never want to go through again. If it wasn't for Scott and Russell, I don't know what might have happened. My best friends deserve medals for what I put them through."

"I find that very hard to believe. You are strong and competent, with a touch of arrogance and conceit," she added with a smile.

"You know me so well." He cradled her soft face in his hands. She'd gotten more beautiful, if that was possible. "It took a while for me to get where I am today. Until I returned to Laurel Heights, there was a part of me that needed mending. You and your love healed me completely, Jessie." Technically she was still on duty, despite being in plain clothes, but he didn't care. He lowered his lips and gave her a sweet kiss that lasted a lot longer than either intended.

"Where is Preston?" Cindi asked the moment Lincoln and Jessie came into view.

"He needed some time alone," Lincoln said to both women. "Jen, your brother will pick you up at ten tomorrow morning and take you to breakfast at the Spoonful." He turned to Cindi Pearl and delivered the cold, unfeeling message.

"Preston said he'd call you."

Cindi's heart and face suffered an invisible, painful blow. What more could she expect? "It's my fault," she blubbered as fresh tears ran down her face. "I never should have suggested all the pomp and circumstance for the dedication." She threw her pretty white hat to the ground and stomped on the crown. "Once again, I went full steam ahead without thinking and embarrassed him."

"No you didn't!" Jennie Reynolds gave Cindi a comforting hug. "Men can be heartless shits, my brother included, and he needed a swift kick in his ass. The entire program was beautifully done."

"I should look for him and apologize."

Jessie, Lincoln and Jennie shouted "No!" at the same time.

"Give him time to brood and think." Lincoln picked up her dented hat and plopped it on her head. "A little dilapidated. Doesn't look too bad." He winked.

"I know a good way to lift our spirits," Jen said. "How about some fireworks?"

"Good idea," Jessie agreed. "My mother and Edie are saving our places down by the lake."

Preston called himself every kind of fool as he sat on a fallen tree limb, hidden in the shadows by the lake, watching the sky fill with giant sunbursts of colors and shooting stars. He was totally oblivious to the boom of the explosions. He had a perfect view of Cindi sitting on a blanket with her arm around Edie. They shared a bowl of popcorn and pulled puffs of cotton candy from clear bags. His sister sat next to Margaret Taylor, deep in conversation. Lincoln and Jessie were wrapped in a blanket, and not all of their attention was on the fireworks. He'd strongly debated joining the others, but needed this time to reflect on the past hour. His emotions were in turmoil, but he felt lighter around the heart. He still harbored serious issues, but changes were needed in his life. Cindi Pearl Sullivan was number one on his list.

Cindi forced a laugh at something Edie had just related about an incident that happened in Sunday school. She deserved an academy award for her performance. Inside, a huge ache surrounded her heart, and she was crying silent tears. Preston was hurting because of her. Oh, how she'd wanted to go after him and confess her duplicity and beg his forgiveness, but most of all, she wanted to comfort him.

She turned her head and scanned the darkened wooded area off the lake. Her eyes paused, catching an unusual shadow lower to the ground. It was too solid to be foliage. Every bone in her body said it was him. Not giving a second thought to her action, she raised her fingers to her lips and blew him a kiss.

He raised his hand and caught the loving gesture. The warmth in her phantom kiss melted the lingering coldness around his heart.

CHAPTER 7

The sun was peaking over the horizon when Samantha Kingsley headed for the equipment shed that doubled as a five-unit garage. Mondays were always busy, so she wanted to get to the Spoonful a little early to try a new recipe: glazed donut muffins, a breakfast treat she planned to offer in her new shop. She'd been quite specific in how she wanted her Victorian-themed tea shop to appear. As a personal favor, Russell Long, Lincoln's best friend and an award-winning architect, had brought her dream to life. The elaborate blueprints had been approved by the Laurel Heights Planning Board, and Sam Morlock agreed to oversee the extensive renovations on the double storefront adjacent to the Spoonful Café. Sallie Mae was delighted to sell the vacant space for Samantha's new business. If all went as planned, the grand opening would be on Valentine's Day the following year.

The July sun promised to deliver another hot day, and sweat covered her brow. On days like this, she strongly debated cutting her champagne-blond hair, currently twisted in a long braid. Her thin cotton pants and white T-shirt were comfortable to wear while cooking behind a hot grill.

She pushed the button to unlock her Jeep four-by-four, but stopped short at the sight of Pansy, Cindi Pearl's pride and joy. The light orchid body of the VW had been defaced with orange and black spray paint. The perp either was illiterate or had purposely misspelled the curse words and ugly personal insults. Samantha's Jeep, Harley and truck hadn't been touched. First the stuffed animal, then the garbage and now this. It was obvious someone had a score to settle with Cindi and knew enough about her personal life to single out her vehicle. Sam's concern for her best friend's welfare had just tripled.

Personal life! "Oh, shit! They'd gone specifically for Cindi's vehicle, but what about Donut and the rest of the animals? Immediate panic had her racing over the concrete driveway toward the barn. She threw open the wooden door to the ground level. Her sigh of relief cut through the quiet interior. Brownie was sucking at her mother's udder. Cookie and Cream Puff were in their nesting box. Cupcake, Muffin and Donut were nowhere in sight.

"You guys had better be enjoying an early morning swim," Sam muttered, jogging over the thick layer of newly mown grass and down the short dirt path to the large pond fed by underground artesian wells. The rays of the birthing sun danced on the gentle ripples, and the tall green reeds and brown cattails swayed in the slight morning breeze.

"Cupcake, Muffin, Donut," she called. Nothing. Normally they'd respond when she called their name. Sam's worries intensified. "Come on, guys, don't do this to me." She hurried down the small wooden dock and searched the rowboat and two paddle craft. The first time she'd found them in the rowboat, she'd laughed, imagining them portraying Wynkin, Blynkin and Nod from the child's nursery rhyme.

Sam circled the water's edge, brushing aside the shoulder-high reeds and stopped short when she noticed two pink bows caught up on a thick stem. "No! No," she shrieked and kicked off her sneakers before rushing into the water that came up to her knees. Alongside the pink ribbons was Donut's black-and-white-check bow tie. Sickness filled her belly and tears were already running down Samantha's face.

She hurried back to dry land and frantically searched the surface of the water, praying she wouldn't spot any white feathers. She'd gotten the sisters when they were ducklings. Cupcake and Muffin were the babies she could never have. Desperation had her calling their names, as she made her way back to the house, clutching the ribbons and bow tie. "Cupcake! Muffin! Donut!"

Cindi turned her head on her down-filled pillow and blinked at the light of the new day that pierced her bedroom windowpanes. The gentle breeze fluttered the lacy white panels on the three open windows. She loved her room under the high eaves and had chosen the four-poster bed along with an orchid-and-white Amish quilt to create an atmosphere of country charm. Her bedroom was on the second floor, where the temperature was always hotter, but the stone house fought off the summer heat. She loved this time of morning, when everything was fresh and new.

Saturday's debacle crept into her waking thoughts. The day had been almost perfect, but ended in despair. Preston had texted a short message Sunday afternoon, apologizing for his rude behavior, but said nothing else. She yearned to take him in her arms and make his pain go away, but that wasn't about to happen anytime soon, if ever. Not even the sight of her new sundress, with small, pale blue–and–purple forget-me-knots, hanging on her closet door, could raise her spirits.

She was just about to head into the shower when she heard Samantha calling out to their pets. It was the panic in her voice that said something was very wrong. She grabbed her robe from the cedar chest at the bottom of her bed, threw it on to cover her nightgown, and hurried down the stairs.

"What's going on?" Cindi cried just as Samantha rushed into the kitchen. "Why are you holding the ducks' ribbons and Donut's bow tie? And you're all wet."

"They were in the reeds, and the three amigos are nowhere to be found. That isn't all. Someone did a job on Pansy with cans of orange and black spray paint. You'd better take a look. I already checked on the other animals and they're fine."

Cindi quickly stepped into her cowgirl boots and tightened the belt on her robe, hurrying after Samantha to the equipment shed. The ugly graffiti stopped her dead in her tracks. "The damn bastards defiled my girl and they can't even spell right! Enough is enough. We're calling the police."

"I agree. You call headquarters, and I'm going to look for our babies."

"Wait! I have idea. We don't have a bloodhound, but I'll bet Cookie can find them. That ornery rooster is as free-spirited as they are and Cupcake, Muffin and Donut are his buddies. If they're on the property, Cookie will find them."

"Good idea," Samantha said, as they headed for the barn.

"I can't believe we are using the rooster as a bloodhound," Cindi said, collecting the feed from the bin. "Cookie can be stubborn, but he never refuses food."

"Cindi, none of our animals act normal. We've got a pygmy goat that wears a bow tie and likes to belly flop into the water. Cookie loves to strut around wearing his little top hat. Our prissy female ducks aren't happy unless they are wearing pink bows. They like peanut butter cookies and chill out on a rug in front of a fire. I'll contact Sallie Mae to let her know I'll be late and why. At the rate gossip flies, we'll be lucky if the entire town doesn't show up to search for our missing pets."

"Sam, think about what you just said. That means whoever did this isn't from around here."

No one questioned Cindi's unusual reason for calling in the Laurel Heights police to search for a missing pygmy goat and two ducks. The threesome was popular with everyone, especially Edith Amanda Adams, the lieutenant's daughter. In the end, two cars showed up. The officers took a report on the damage to her vehicle before they set the rooster loose.

"Go find your buddies," Samantha coaxed Cookie, tossing feed on the ground outside the confinement of the barn. The rooster stopped to cock-a-doodle a number of times at his human search party to let everyone know he was in charge, before heading for the cornfields that bordered her property.

Dixie Bell Grote, recently promoted to sergeant, raised a brow. "You've got to be kidding. We're supposed to put our faith in a cocky rooster wearing a top hat and follow him through cornstalks that are higher than our heads?"

"Don't knock it. He's the best we've got." Cindi said, wishing she'd had time to go into the house and put on her jeans before heading into the cornfield. "Go, Cookie, go!"

"This is a corn maze, so everyone stay together," Sergeant Grote ordered as Laurel Heights' finest followed Cookie, cock-a-doodle-doing all the way.

A half hour later, they found the missing critters close to the newly installed natural gas pumps. The ducks started quacking in answer to Cookie's alert that help was on the way. Someone had confined them in three animal carriers. After a very tearful reunion and being subjected to a thorough going-over by their human mothers, the critters enjoyed peanut butter cookies and decided they'd had enough adventures for one day. They took refuge in the house on the rug in front of the cold hearth.

It was late morning when Cindi finally made it into the office. She really wanted to talk to Lincoln, but he was in a private meeting with his door closed. She was halfway through checking her e-mail messages, when his office door opened. Jessie, in full uniform, walked out.

"Are you all right?" Jessie's voice was filled with concern. "Laurel Heights is all abuzz with what happened to your animals. Edie heard the transmission on my police radio before she went to the soccer camp they are having at the middle school. She was upset and announced she had to go to the farm and help look for the critters. As soon as I learned they were safe, I called the school and had them send a message to Edie that all was well."

"What about your car?" Lincoln asked.

"I've already notified my insurance company and let them know I've filed a police report. Paul's Garage towed Pansy into Stevensville to the body repair shop. I'm using Sam's Jeep, and she used her Harley to get to work."

"I sent a crew out there to upgrade the exterior security." Lincoln said. "There will be twenty-four-hour surveillance on all the outbuildings."

Jessie stood in front of Cindi's desk. "This situation has gotten out of control. I'm going to add the garbage incident and the criminal mischief to your vehicle to the file I started on the embezzlement of funds. I'll also include the stuffed animal episode. Detective Donnelly will be contacting you for a follow-up investigation."

"My first instinct is to argue with you, but this is out of my hands. I hope it doesn't get out and we lose volunteers and supporters. We are so close to completing the track. They are hooking up the utilities to the concession stand and restrooms at the end of the week. The bleachers and reviewing stand are being delivered and installed next week, along with the marquee. I have to talk to the other board members, but I don't know who to trust, other than my brother and the people in this room."

"Cindi, this is going to happen. The supplemental account is already set up so you can pay the distributors and contractors on your signature. You've set a date for the dedication next month and we are not disappointing those children." Lincoln sighed heavily. It had been a morning and a half. He tapped the brim of his wife's cap. "I need a boost of caffeine. Can I talk you into joining me for coffee?"

"No thanks. I've got to get back to work. I just wanted to stop by and tell you about the plumbing problem in the garage. Preston is not going to like living in the Last Chance Motel."

"Why will I have to move to the motel?" Preston asked, walking into Cindi's office. Guilt had him avoiding all eye contact with her.

"I was just about to call you," Lincoln said. "My darling wife stopped by to tell me they had to shut the water off in your apartment. After you left this morning, my mother-in-law went into the garage and noticed water running down the side wall. Two pipes burst, and the plumber said the repair job is going to be quite extensive because all the galvanized pipes should be replaced."

"That means I'll be homeless for a while." Preston pursed his lips. "I really don't want to stay in the motel. I could always bunk in my office."

"What about the finished space above Sam's barn?" Lincoln looked at Cindi. "Do you think she'd mind if Preston stayed there till the repairs are made in the apartment?"

"I don't see why not, but you would have to get Samantha's permission since it's her property. The only furniture is a bed."

Jessie patted her husband's cheek. "I knew I married a smart man."

"I can eat here since the cafeteria is open twenty-four/seven," Preston said. "There is always the Spoonful or Jack's Pizza or his new Trattoria. I won't starve."

"I'll call Samantha right now," Lincoln volunteered and pulled out his cell phone.

This was happening too fast, Cindi decided, studying the three people in her office. They were more like actors on a stage. They talked too fast and their lines were perfectly executed. This plumbing problem needed a little more investigating. Her heart beat a little faster when she realized Preston would be living so close.

"We're all set." Lincoln grinned. "Samantha thought it was a great idea, and I told her my workers were already at the farm, upgrading security. She has plenty of bed linens and towels."

"Looks like I have new digs." Preston enjoyed a secret smile. Step one had gone more smoothly than he'd anticipated.

"Can you stick around for a few minutes?" Lincoln asked. "There is something I need to discuss with both of you. First let me walk Jessie to her car."

"No problem."

Preston adjusted the knot on his blue paisley tie that really didn't need adjusting and shoved his hands in the pockets of bullet-gray dress slacks. Step two, asking for Cindi's forgiveness, wasn't going to be as easy. The hours he'd spent alone in the woods Saturday evening had given him time to think about his life. Cindi had been right when she said he was selfish and didn't care about anyone but himself. He'd enclosed himself in his own hellish world, shutting his parents and sister out of his life.

Cindi couldn't stand the lingering silence that filled her sun-brightened office, so she spoke up. "Did your sister get off okay?"

"Yes. She said to tell you to keep in touch and she couldn't wait to move to Laurel Heights."

"Jennie gave me her card with her e-mail address."

"The green streaks in your hair are gone," he blurted, searching his brain for the right words.

Cindi brushed a nervous finger down the length of her hair. "Finally."

"It's a good thing you got rid of them, or the Jolly Green Giant might have fallen in love."

"I'm not that lucky." Cindi smirked.

"You removed the tattoo."

She glanced down at her bare arm, disappointed that he never got a chance to nibble on the lollipop. "It came off after a good scrubbing." This small talk added to her frustration, and she reached for her Slinky.

I never did get a chance to nibble on it, he silently noted and began to pace. There was so much he wanted to say, but he didn't know where to begin. "Cindi, I—" he started, but she cut him off.

"I owe you an apology," she blurted, just as the Slinky slipped out of her hands and rolled under her desk. She bent down to retrieve the toy and knocked her head on the underside of the desk. "Ouch." She winced, rubbing the back of her head.

"Are you okay?"

"I'll live." Why did she always appear to be a klutz in front of him?

"Back to my original question. Why do you owe me an apology?"

"It was my idea to have the special ceremony on Saturday night. I should have told you beforehand. But once again, I put you in an embarrassing position."

Cindi Pearl was his first priority in making necessary changes in his life. He walked around her desk and put his hands on her shoulders. She was trembling. "No, you are wrong," he said softly. "I owe *you* an apology for running off. The ceremony was beautiful and touching, and I was proud to stand beside Lincoln and honor those who served with us. Saturday night helped me face and accept quite a few things in my life. I've finally accepted that I have a form of post-traumatic stress disorder. I need to resolve a few issues and plan to talk to one of the psychologists on staff." He shifted his hands to her face. The sun had brought out the few freckles on her cheeks. "You helped me do something that I haven't done in a very long time. I laughed, really laughed and joked with my sister. My smile and laugh were genuine, not forced. So you see, Cindi Pearl Sullivan, I should be thanking you." He tipped her head forward and kissed the raised lump on her head. "All better."

"Best medicine in the world," she said with a heart-melting smile. *Too bad I didn't bang my mouth.*

"Do you have a problem with me living in the loft apartment in the barn?"

His neck was the perfect place to rest her cheek as her arms slid around him. He felt so good, so damned good. "No, I'll like having you close. And thank you, thank you, for not being angry with me. I just wanted you to know how special you are." *To me*, she silently continued. "I know you don't want to hear it, but I need a hero to help me get through all the problems I'm facing." Cindi didn't care that she was babbling. "I was scared to death when we couldn't find Cupcake, Muffin and Donut this morning. I wish you had been there. My car is another problem."

"What are you talking about?" Preston's arms drew her closer. She felt so good, so damned good.

"I thought you might have heard, since it's all over town." Cindi told him about the kidnapping and the graffiti on her car. "The stupid idiot called me a whore and cunt and spelled it *count* and *hor* along with a bunch of other curses."

"The bastard!" Preston wanted to take her mind off her worries with a loving kiss, but he hadn't earned the privilege. "I'm sorry I wasn't there, but that is about to change, as of this evening. Any chance you can give me a hand moving my stuff?"

"I'd be glad to." Cindi raised her head from his shoulder. "I was sorry you didn't get to see the fireworks."

"Oh, I saw them," he admitted with a genuine grin.

Cindi's heart leaped with gladness when his smile reached his eyes. "I wasn't wrong! I saw a dark shape, like a person sitting close to the ground. My heart—I mean, my gut," she quickly corrected herself, "said it was you. Were you watching us?"

"Yes." *So I was right thinking my feelings aren't one-sided.*

"Why didn't you join us?"

"I wasn't ready," Preston truthfully admitted.

Cindi put her hands to her hot cheeks. "That means you saw what I did."

Preston lifted his fisted hand. "I caught it, but Cindi Pearl, I intend to collect."

She reached for his other hand, kissed his palm and folded his fingers closed. "Now you have two."

Lincoln chose that moment to return and grinned. "It's about damn time." He continued into his office but didn't close the door. "When you two are finished playing kissy-face, I need Preston first and then Cindi Pearl."

CHAPTER 8

Cindi glanced in the rearview mirror, checking to see if Preston was still behind her. After work, they'd stopped by the apartment and packed up his clothes and few personal belongings. She'd volunteered to collect the toiletries from the bathroom. Sure enough, there was a good-size hole in the wall under the sink, exposing old galvanized water pipes. Two of the connections had been removed, so the water problem wasn't a fabrication. Sam had called earlier to say the bed had been made and the place was livable. Cindi asked what Sam meant by livable. Samantha only laughed.

When she turned down the drive, two older pickup trucks and a minivan she recognized as Sallie Mae's, were parked to the side of the barn. She managed to pull around the vehicles and stop in the equipment shed. Preston parked his Aston Martin in Pansy's spot.

"What's going on?" he asked the moment he stepped out of his car.

"Beats me. Come on. Let's find Samantha."

As was his habit, he took her hand, and they headed for the barn. The double doors were wide open and two men walked up the ramp, balancing a rolled-up carpet on their shoulders.

"Are you having some kind of rummage sale?"

"If we are, no one told me," Cindi said.

They found Sam sitting in one of the wicker rocking chairs on the side porch, drinking a glass of iced sweet tea. Sallie Mae occupied the other chair and munched on a large chocolate chip cookie.

"Are we having a garage sale no one told me about?" Cindi helped herself to one of her favorite cookies and, as an afterthought, passed one to Preston. They'd never stopped for dinner.

"It's just the opposite," Sallie Mae said. "When the town found out Preston had to move into the unfurnished apartment, everyone decided to pool extra pieces of furniture."

"People have been arriving since I got home from work," Samantha added.

"Everyone brought me furniture?" Preston couldn't get over the town's generosity. "Is that okay with you?"

"I have lived here long enough to know that when the people of Laurel Heights want to help out someone in need, they cannot be put off," Samantha said. "When you move out, people will pick up their donations so they can be used for the next guy. Think of it as rent-free furniture. Are you ready to see your new apartment?"

Sallie Mae pushed up from the wicker armchair. "I'm going to head home. Call Northrup if you need anything else, and he'll open the store." She kissed Preston on the cheek. "I am very proud of you, my boy." Then she whispered something in his ear.

He smiled and nodded in return.

"What was that all about?" Cindi asked.

"That's between Sallie Mae and me."

Preston shook hands with the two men who were just leaving and thanked them for their help. The women held back and suggested he go up the stairs first. When he got to the previously bare space, his mouth dropped open in wonderment. What they'd done to make the place livable was mind-boggling.

The furniture fairies had set up a makeshift kitchen in one corner of the room. A square table, inset with black-and-white mosaic tiles and four white ladder-back chairs, sat atop a woven area rug in a rainbow of colors. A sky-blue vase, filled with pale pink mountain laurel flowers, sat in the center of the table beside a wood napkin holder. They'd filled the apple-shaped caddy with white paper napkins. A small microwave, electric teapot and coffee maker sat atop a waist-high white cabinet. The open doors revealed an assortment of mugs, plates and eating utensils and a set of salt-and-pepper shakers in the shape of Siamese cats. Someone had donated a bar-size refrigerator.

The so-called living room's designer must have been color-blind or had a panic attack. A seashell-pink fan-back chair shared a corner with a square end table that matched the green streaks in Cindi's hair. The table lamp had been made from a lava light, currently spitting kelly-green globs. The black-and-white stripes on a mustard-gold chair rivaled the pelt of a jungle tiger. An oval glass table, supported by refinished driftwood, fronted the persimmon-colored couch with black picture frame arms. They'd finished off the living room by adding a burnt-orange-and-gold area rug patterned in exploding sunbursts.

"Oh my God! This is unbelievable!" Cindi cried.

Preston took a hesitant step into the psychedelic-themed room. "I'm afraid to enter the bedroom."

"You are pretty safe," Sam assured him, trying not to laugh. "I donated the white pine night tables and dresser. The two wrought iron bed lamps were made by the same blacksmith who designed the ornate lights in the barn. They managed to put an old stuffed armchair in one corner. It's actually quite comfortable. I made up the bed and put towels in the bathroom. Anything else you'll have to pick up on your own."

Preston turned about and gave his new living quarters a cursory inspection. It was going to take getting used to. "I am truly overwhelmed."

It was the sound of a cuckoo clock that was their undoing, and they burst out laughing. Overwhelmed by the sight of the cacophony of furniture, they had failed to notice the wooden Black Forest clock on the wall beside the stairs. Below the clock, the furniture donation committee had hung a handmade needlepoint sign that read, "Home Sweet Home."

To celebrate his new living quarters, Preston volunteered to drive into town and pick up dinner and a bottle of red wine. They opted for a loaded pizza and an antipasto from Jack's Pizzeria. Mrs. Flach, the owner's wife, added a couple of napoleons, one of her specialty pastries.

They enjoyed dinner sitting on the side porch. Preston felt relaxed, and right at home, especially in the company of two beautiful women. "Thank you for letting me stay here. I insist on paying some kind of rent, and don't argue with me."

"We'll work something out, but we appreciate you being here to help keep an eye on things." Samantha didn't remind Preston she was well trained in hand-to-hand and re-qualified in weaponry every six months. She stood up and downed the rest of her wine. "Thanks for the dinner. I'm going to check on the critters and then go to bed. Have a good evening and don't stay up too late."

"Yes, Mom," Cindi teased.

Flickering candles, protected by two glass chimneys, gave off a soft glow, and the gentle breeze moved the heavy evening air. Cindi pressed a hand to her very full stomach. "I don't know about you, but I'd like to take a walk."

"Me too. Any special place you like to go?"

"The pond is my favorite place on the property. There is a bench so we can sit by the water. Some nights, Sam and I build a fire in the man-made fire pit, so we can make s'mores."

No sooner had they stepped off the porch when something butted his shin. Fortunately, Donut chose Preston's left leg. "We have a chaperone."

"Cupcake and Muffin won't be far behind. You will soon realize that the three amigos rule the roost around here. Cookie, our rooster, hangs out with them during the day, but prefers to stay in the barn with Cream Puff, his main squeeze, when it's dark."

"I better mind my p's and q's." Preston reached for her hand when they walked up the slate-lined path between the buildings and made their way to the pond. "Tell me about your family and something about Cindi Pearl that isn't in a standard personnel file. Don't bother to tell me your favorite color. I already know." He grinned.

"Okay, but you have to do the same. My parents live on the outskirts of Stevensville on a small farm. They have a few chickens and a huge vegetable garden. They are both retired and love to go flea marketing. My older brother Denny and his wife have three children. He's a truck driver and lives down the road from my parents. As a kid, I dreamed of becoming a ballet dancer, but the first time I tried to go up on my toes, my ankles gave out and I broke my little toe. I thought about becoming an astronaut, but I went on a roller coaster and threw up. Heights and excessive g's definitely didn't agree with me. For a time, I thought about becoming a veterinarian, so my mother suggested I volunteer at an animal shelter. One of my jobs was to clean up the poop. It was so gross. Again, I threw up."

Preston couldn't help but laugh. "Are you making this up?"

"Nope. You wanted to know something about me that wasn't written down. My mother has pictures of me throwing up after the amusement ride if you want proof. Okay, enough about me."

"My career aspirations weren't as colorful as yours. I grew up in Oregon and my parents still live in Newport. My father is a marine biologist and is one of the head honchos at the marine science center. He's spent a great deal of his life studying dolphins. My parents met in college, fell in love and got married. My mother's parents are very well-off and were appalled their daughter chose to ignore her college education to marry and raise a family."

"Do they still feel that way?"

"No, they've come around and think the world of my father. I loved surfing and water-skiing, anything that had to do with water."

"Is that where you earned the name Dolphin?"

"Yes, but how did you find out about my nickname?"

"Your sister told me."

"It was a long time ago."

Cindi caught the wistful regret in his voice, and it made her more determined to make him realize he could do those things again if he really tried. "If you loved the water so much, why didn't you follow in your father's footsteps?"

"At the time, my main goal in life was to have fun, but I was always a wiz with numbers. My grandfather on my mother's side, claimed I inherited the skill from him. When I was twenty, he gave me fifty thousand dollars and challenged me to double the money in six months."

"Did you win?"

"I made ten times the amount and gave him back his original fifty thousand plus ten percent. I discovered a new way to have fun. Over the years, I've made some very wise investments and built up quite a nest egg."

"Now I know how you are able to drive an Aston Martin."

"Guilty, but now I have fun tracking down other people's ill-gotten gains."

They reached the pond and sat on the wooden bench. Overhead, the black velvet sky was brilliant with twinkling stars, and the light from the summer moon danced on the gentle waves. Frogs croaked among the swaying reeds, and fireflies flickered through the air. A gaggle of geese joined Cupcake and Muffin for a swim.

"I love it here." Cindi cradled Donut in her lap and snuggled against Preston when he draped his arm about her shoulder. "Except for the night creatures, everything is so peaceful and quiet."

"Why do you think I wanted to transfer from Manhattan to Laurel Heights?" For now he'd keep it to himself that he wanted to be near her.

Two geese chose that moment to come in for a landing and gracefully glide across the calm water, giving Cindi an idea. "Do you miss water sports?"

"Yes. I miss skiing in the winter, too. Notice I didn't clam up or cringe at the question?"

Cindi was thrilled by his positive attitude and pressed a little more. "We could drive to Henry Long's campground, just outside of town. They offer ski and boat rentals. In the winter there are wonderful slopes in the area that have all kinds of winter sports."

The gently bobbing rowboat drew his attention. "We could take a ride in that little dinghy some night. I'm great at rowing."

"Some nights, when it's hot, I go swimming. The water is quite warm."

When there wasn't a response, Cindi lifted her head and noticed he was staring at his closed fist. "Is something wrong?"

"Do you know what I'm holding in my hand?"

She did, but played stupid. "No."

"Something sweet and wonderful that I really want to collect."

Her heart beat a little faster. "I believe you have two treasures on account. I forgot to mention that the longer it takes you to collect, the more the interest builds up."

He tightened his arm and lifted her chin with a finger. Moonlight highlighted her natural beauty. "You never mentioned a penalty. What's the percentage?"

"A hundred percent. Kiss for kiss. You better hurry up and start collecting. The interest is building up as we speak."

"Numbers men hate interest, but this is one time I'll gladly pay." He lowered his head and captured her upturned mouth. Luscious, heavenly lips eagerly blended with his. When her arm came up and wrapped around his neck, he sunk in further. Precious, sweet Cindi Pearl.

Donut wanted nothing to do with the human's lovey-dovey cuddling and jumped off her lap. "That's one," Preston murmured, lowered his head a second time and took the kiss a whole lot deeper.

When he finally let her up for air, he sampled the tender skin under her jaw. "Let me know when I've erased all the penalties."

Cindi met his skimming lips and softly moaned, "I forgot to mention that for every penalty paid within the allotted time, you get bonus points, but there is a time limit, so you'd better get back to clearing up your debt."

"Gladly."

That was the start of their nightly routine: after-dinner walks, rowboat rides and kisses, lots and lots of kisses. When he asked Cindi if he'd cleared up his debt, she just said he was getting close. Some nights Samantha joined them for pizza.

Other nights they dined alone at the Laurel Bistro. One night he used Samantha's kitchen and prepared Jennie's chicken pot pie. His sister prided herself on the recipe and gave Preston explicit instructions.

In between his priority work for Adams Security, Preston worked on tracking the theft from the derby fund. He'd put a call in to Reggie DeWitt, their head computer tech in the Manhattan office, to track the package. Preston uncovered the initial theft, but did further research on the person and was troubled by what he'd uncovered. Each time he checked another account, it opened another can of worms. In his opinion, there was no simple fix. Cindi was not going to like what he'd found.

Preston glanced at the time on his watch and realized he'd better get a move on. It was already after four and he had a stop to make before he went home. He'd been living on the farm for a week and he no longer found pleasure in working after hours. There was someone waiting. The thought gave him untold happiness. He'd also promised Cindi they would visit the Laurel Heights Campground after dinner to check out the boat rentals.

He tossed his glasses onto his desk and rubbed his tired eyes. His nightly walks with Cindi were becoming more frustrating. One touch, one caress and things heated up between them like a wood-stoked fire. The other night things had gotten hot and heavy. When she took off her tank top and bared her beautiful breasts, it was all he could do not to strip off the rest of her clothes. Maybe it was time to take a little breather. What the hell kind of excuse would he give? *Get real, PJ. You couldn't make it through the day without her. You are hopelessly in love with Cindi Pearl.*

A half hour later, the haunting sounds of Sophie Tucker singing "Some of These Days" came from overhead speakers when Preston walked into the doggie hotel on Main Street. In the early nineteen hundreds, The Hotel was the only place travelers could stay since it was a block from the train station. Buford Adams, Lincoln Adams's late grandfather, had purchased the building slated for demolition. After restoring the interior to its original turn-of-the-century beauty, he was approached by the town veterinarian. Dr. Dubielsky opened the pet clinic, doggie day care and spa. The shop would be closing in ten minutes, so he wasn't surprised it was empty. He walked down one of the Persian carpet runners that protected the dark mahogany floors and headed toward the veterinary section off the main room. A female voice was raised in anger. Someone was getting chewed out.

"Just like a man! Can't control your dick! With the swish of tail, you fall for a sexy piece of ass. You've got a perfectly good woman at home. You're a cheater! You better pray those babies have pure white hair! I should have had you neutered, but I didn't want you to be a eunuch!"

Preston stopped in the doorway of the examining room. Lisa Kay, the vet tech, stood in front of a metal table and waived a sheet of paper in front of a black cat that totally ignored her tirade. Her blue smock with happy dogs and cats topped straight-leg jeans. He knew her to be in her early forties and she was engaged to Sam Morlock, a billionaire by inheritance, but a contractor and carpenter by choice. She also lived next door to Jessie and Lincoln.

"I take it he cheated on Abby Lincoln, Edie's cat." Preston stepped into the brightly lit room, and it took all of his self-control not to laugh. Xavier Cugat continued to lick his paws.

His nonchalant manner infuriated Lisa Kay that much more. She turned away from the horny womanizer and shook the legal document. "He couldn't pick an ordinary cat to poke with his pecker! No, he went after Simone, a white Angora cat. This is an official notice from the owner. If it turns out Don Juan is the father, I'll have to pay for the kittens. Do you know how much they cost? It's a good thing my Sam has money!"

"Look at it this way. The owner won't be able to make you pay full price because they won't be purebred."

"There is that," she laughed. "I got your e-mail about adding an animal to the menagerie at Samantha's farm and contacted Nicola Harding. She is moving to London and was relieved her pet would be going to a good family. Dr. Dubielsky has been taking care of the donkey since she was a couple of months old and is familiar with her needs. I'll make arrangements to bring the donkey to the farm, along with a supply of feed and care instructions."

"Perfect. Remember, it's a surprise. Aren't you going to ask why I'm interested in this particular rescue animal?"

Lisa Kay perched on the hip-high examining table and lifted Xavier Cugat in her arms. She ran a hand over his soft black coat. "Not really. It takes out-of-the-ordinary people to open their hearts to animals with unique needs. I consider you a very special person, but I do have one question. Are you doing this for yourself or for Cindi Pearl? Most guys send girls flowers or candy to show their love."

The blush that swept across his cheeks would be contrary to denying her accusation. He stepped closer to the table and ran a hand over Xavier Cugat's head. "I'm going to take the Fifth on your question, but feel free to make your own determination."

"Good enough. You couldn't find a better person to entrust with your heart."

"I know," he mumbled on his way out the door. Lisa Kay never heard his reply.

"It's a beautiful evening. I'm so glad we decided to eat out on the porch. Preston should be coming home any time." Cindi placed red-and-white-checked napkins on the glass-topped picnic table.

"That sounds so domestic," Samantha teased, lightly tossing a bowl of fresh greens from their garden that she'd laced with her special lemon-lime vinaigrette dressing. "The grilled veggies are done, and the steaks won't take long because the grill is hot." Sam sat down in one of the white wicker chairs and picked up her glass of cabernet. "Has he made love to you yet?"

"You mean, has he taken off like a jackhammer?"

"What!" Samantha almost choked on her wine. "Tell me more."

Cindi explained about the private joke she'd shared with Jennie Reynolds. "I don't know what is stopping him. When we are down by the pond, sometimes I straddle his lap and rub myself against him. He's hot, rock-hard and so ready. The other night, I took off my tank and was surprised spittle didn't drip from his mouth. I was naked and had high hopes he'd lose control. He suckled my breasts like a starving man who'd gotten his first taste of food in years. Then he stopped! I couldn't have been hotter if they served me up on a spit at a luau! I was so frustrated, I dove into the pond to cool off. Donut jumped in after me. You know what PJ did?"

"I wasn't there, remember?" Sam folded her lips, trying to hold in her laugh.

"He laughed, really laughed! So I stood up in all my half-naked glory and tossed handfuls of water at him. He finally stopped laughing and offered me his shirt. We were almost back to the barn when he whispered in my ear that I taste delicious and my wet breasts look beautiful in the moonlight. I never knew a man to have so much self-control. From now on I'm going to limit his touchy-feely action. If enough frustration builds up, he'll finally jump my bones."

Sam decided a change of subject was needed. "Have you asked him to go with you to the soap box derby in Stevensville? Better yet, have you made your special arrangements?"

"I called in a couple of favors, so we're set. I'm going to ask him after dinner. We're driving out to Henry Long's campground to deliver the box of cookies you made for Billy Landis. The kid will figure out soon enough that it's his parent's way of checking up on him.

Preston drove his sleek car down a curvy road through a thick-forested area that led to the campground bordering Laurel Lake. Signs and trail markers, supported by carved wood black bears, provided directions to the different sections of the prime piece of real estate.

"I didn't realize this place was so big." Preston slowed and took the fork to the marina.

"Along with the tent and trailer sites, there are fully furnished rental cabins, a clubhouse, a concession stand, general store and a gift shop. Henry recently added a second pool, kid-friendly, and another playground for the children. Once the new Laurel Heights Inn is completed, the cabins will be available year-round. Each one has its own stone fireplace and kitchenette. It's not public knowledge, but he's franchised a café that will offer breakfast and lunch."

"Won't that cut into the Spoonful's business?"

"Sallie Mae isn't the least bit worried." Cindi smiled. "It was her idea to open The Tablespoon."

"She is one smart businesswoman. How do you know so much about the place?"

"Again, not for public knowledge. Long and Barrows, Scott and Russell's architectural division, designed the inn, but they, along with Lincoln, invested in Henry's new venture. The details and legal documents come across my desk. They anticipate completion by next summer."

Preston offered a sheepish smile. "Guess you don't know about the second phase, the convention center and pro golf course they plan to build in two years."

"What convention center?" Then it hit her. "You invested in the project too?"

"Russell put me in touch with his father. We discussed how much I'd like to contribute and, as they say, the rest is history. It's an excellent investment. Oh, and Sam Morlock has tossed his hat into the ring. He's even suggested one of the bars resemble a train dining car from the twenties."

Cindi tapped the dashboard with an appreciative hand. "Just as long as you don't lose your shirt and have to sell this great car."

Preston patted the back of her hand. "Have no fear." He kept it to himself that he owned a second one, which he parked at his parents' house. Jennie loved the car and kept the engine well-tuned.

They took a second left at the sign that read "Parking, Boats and Rentals." At this time of night, the huge paved lot was almost empty. Pleasure craft of all sizes were tied up to the mooring docks and bobbed in the gentle swells. A one-story building, painted turquoise-blue, bordered the water's edge. The white shutters on the retail windows had been lowered for the day.

Cindi grabbed the round tin of cookies she'd set on the backseat and got out of the car. "Billy Landis is working at the marina for the summer. Fishing is his life, so he must be ecstatic to be around water and be able to fish anytime he wants." She scanned the dock area that included a double-wide boat ramp directly into the lake. "Speak of the devil. See that tall, slender teenager with the fishing pole in his hand? That's Scott and Julie's son." Cindi was glad she wore lightweight pants and a long-sleeve sweater. The early evening breeze off the water made goose bumps blossom on her arms.

"Any new fish tales?" she teased when they got to the end of the long wooden dock.

"Hey, Ms. Cindi! How are you?" he asked with a big smile. The light wind ruffled the sixteen-year-old's dark brown hair, which was in need of a trim. The sun had cast a golden tan on his skin. His still wore a red bathing suit, and the front of his T-shirt displayed a picture of bass fishing boat. "I knew Mom would figure out a way to check on me."

"I wouldn't put it that way. Bill, I'd like you to meet Preston Reynolds. We work together." Cindi held out the can. "Samantha sent you double chocolate fudge and raisin oatmeal cookies."

His golden brown eyes lit up with pleasure. "Fantastic!" He balanced the tin of cookies in one hand and shook hands with the other. "Hey, Mr. Reynolds. The food here is pretty decent, but nothing like homemade cookies. Ms. Samantha bakes as good as my mom."

"Call me Preston. How's the fishing?"

"Not bad, now that my number-one pest went to the gift shop."

Cindi raised a brow. "Pest?"

"Yeah, Edie Adams. Almost every evening she shows up to go fishing. She's got it in her ten-year-old brain she can tell a sixteen-year-old how to fish." Billy's eyes shifted to the walking path that ended dockside. "Speak of the she-devil."

Lisa Kay and Sam Morlock walked hand in hand down a paved path toward the dock. Both wore jeans and nylon windbreakers over their T-shirts. Edie skipped alongside them, wearing a hooded sweatshirt that skimmed the top of her light green shorts. She was babbling about something and slung her arm back and forth like a metronome. In her right hand was a stuffed animal.

The smile on Cindi's face faded and she tightened her grip on Preston's hand. The animal was a replica of the one she'd received with the twisted head.

Preston saw it too and gave her hand a reassuring squeeze. "Don't say anything. We don't want to frighten Edie."

"Funny meeting you here," Sam said, holding out a hand to Preston. "How do you like your new digs?"

"Who can complain when you have two beautiful roommates?"

"Hi, Mr. Reynolds." Edie gave him a quick hug. "It's no fun since you moved out. I don't have anyone to play one-on-one. Daddy works so much. I still can't understand why Mommy had Mr. Morlock punch the big holes in the wall under your sink."

Preston's lips tightened, and he darted a glance at Sam and Lisa Kay. "Out of the mouths of babes."

"Miss Cindi, look what I got! He looks just like Donut." Edie showed her love for the stuffed animal and gave it a hug.

Cindi's attention was focused on the replica of her pygmy goat cradled in Edie's arms, and the "punch holes in the wall" statement never registered in her brain. The sick feeling still hadn't left her stomach, and she forced a smile. "Did you get it in the gift shop?"

"We stopped at the ice cream stand, but the line was out the door. We'll go back in a little while," Lisa said. "We decided to kill some time and made the mistake of going in the gift shop. It is a treasure trove for kids. What are you guys doing here?"

"We came down to check out the type of boat rentals and deliver cookies to Bill." Preston felt Cindi tremble and he slipped a comforting arm around her waist. "Do they have a lot of those particular animals?"

"An entire shelf," Sam said. He'd expected to see a smile on Cindi Pearl's face, but he was confused by her paled features. First the request to put holes in the bathroom wall as an excuse to have Preston move to the farm and now the stuffed animal. Although he took early retirement as an ATF agent, he hadn't lost his ability to sense trouble. He'd put a call in to Lincoln in the morning to find out what the hell was going on.

Preston glanced down at Cindi's colorless cheeks. "Hang in there. What do you say we take a walk through the gift shop too?"

All she did was nod.

Edie chose that moment to tug on Lisa Kay's hand. "I'll bet the line is a lot shorter. Wouldn't it be nice if we asked Billy to have ice cream with us?"

"Would you like to join us?" Sam asked. "It's on me."

Bill Landis was faced with a big decision. Put up with the mouthy "pest" and enjoy free ice cream or decline the invitation. At this point in his teenage life, food took precedent over everything else. "Thanks, that'd be great."

He never did see the giddy, school-girl gleam in Edie's eye.

"See you guys later," Lisa Kay said before giving Preston a knowing wink.

"We don't really have to go in the store," Preston said, as they headed toward the rustic log building that housed the gift shop and concession stand.

"I'm okay. It was just the initial shock of seeing the replica of Donut."

"Do you know if the place has twenty-four-hour security surveillance?"

"You're kidding, right? As soon as we set up the new office and service facility, Henry Long was one of Lincoln's first customers. There's interior and exterior on all buildings and the dock twenty-four/seven."

"How long do they keep the surveillance discs?"

Cindi stopped walking and stared up at Preston with a questioning frown. "You have got to get away from your figures once in a while. Lincoln's company has the latest high-tech equipment. The digital records are kept indefinitely."

"What do you say we give our boss a call and let him know what we've found? Since this is an official investigation, he is authorized to check security records and sales of that item."

"Suppose the person paid cash?"

"Doesn't matter, and it would be in our favor. Not too many people pay cash these days. I'm sure Henry's system is set up to track inventory of every item sold. There will be a record of each sale with a time and a date. Once Linc's e-guys integrate the security tape with the sale of each pygmy goat, we can take a look to see if we recognize the buyer."

"You are so damn smart!" Suddenly Cindi was feeling a whole lot better. She stood on tippy toes and planted a kiss on his delicious mouth. "Let's have a talk with our boss. But first, I want a hot fudge sundae with two cherries on top!"

"Hmm, is one of them for me?" he asked with a hopeful grin.

"I'll make you a deal. If you help me out with another problem, you can have both of them."

Preston pursed his lips. "Is it going to put me in another embarrassing position with your dingbat alter ego?"

"Nope, just the real me. Honest." She made the sign of the cross on her chest.

"I'll take your word, Ms. I-Always-Tell-the-Truth. Your two cherries are mine!"

"Deal!" Her first challenge was to get him to the soap box derby. Convincing him to stay would be another. Maybe she should invest in a jar of cherries.

CHAPTER 9

Three days later, race day had arrived. Today's event was mega-important, not just for the kids, but also for Cindi personally. Once again, she went behind Preston's back and withheld a surprise or two. Seeing and working with the Super Kids could either make or break him. She was also laying her heart on the line. He could wind up hating her.

The sun had barely risen when they left the farm and went for breakfast at the Spoonful. With her stomach already in knots, she should have eaten something light, but the special had been stuffed French toast, one of Samantha's specialties. Preston had eaten the same thing, but added three eggs over easy, plus a side of biscuits and gravy, the house favorite. When the waitress had brought their meals, Samantha sent a note wishing them good luck.

Cindi tried to remain calm and sang along with Bryan Adams as his he crooned, *Everything I do, I do it for you. Ain't that the truth,* she said to herself and glanced at Preston out the corner of her eye as he handled the luxury car with ease. He was going to be hot in those jeans. She'd purposely worn shorts, because the July day promised to live up to its seasonal reputation, hot and humid. If only he would take that stubborn stick out of his cute butt and wear shorts.

"You have a very nice voice, and that is one of my favorite songs."

"Thanks, but I consider myself a shower singer."

He shifted his eyes in her direction and wiggled his eyebrows. "If you ever decide to offer a private performance, I'll buy out the house."

"You'll be the first to know," she offered with an easy laugh. *That will happen when pigs fly.*

"Thank you again for coming with me," she said. "We are always short of volunteers. I'll be on the reviewing stand during the race. You'll get a neon-yellow derby shirt identifying you as staff and a lanyard with a name tag." Cindi spotted their exit on the interstate and put a hand to her nervous stomach. "Take the second exit for Stevensville. The town granted the derby permission to hold the event on Court Street. Driver safety is paramount, and the town blocks off the entire street with horse barriers so no one can go in or out. Residents are given a week's notice to keep their vehicles off the street."

"Thanks, but you already gave me the location and it's programmed in my GPS." Preston wondered why she was so jittery. "How many entrants do you expect?"

Focus, focus. You are not going to throw up. "Fifty applications were submitted. That is considered an average number for a local race. Some meets have a hundred fifty–plus cars. Once the Laurel Heights track is set up, that number will be easy to handle."

Preston moved into the right-hand lane, preparing to exit. "Did you ever drive a soap box car?"

"I'll tell you the truth, but you can't laugh. My brother and I had our own cars, and we raced until we were eighteen. The rules have changed, and kids at the Masters level can drive to the age of twenty. My car was painted a bright yellow and was called The Canary. Somehow or other, I always raced against my brother. It doesn't matter who crosses the finish line first, because you have four chances to race and they average your time. It was our last race and I was in the lead, but something happened to the steering. The car went out of control. I shot up a short ramp and flew into the flags next to the reviewing stand. My brother told everyone I was trying to do my own impersonation of the Amelia Earhart because she named her plane Canary."

"Did you get hurt?'

"Just my pride. I didn't go very high, just took out the flags."

Preston could no longer contain his laugh. "Oh, Cindi Pearl, only you, but I'm a bit confused. If your brother is older and bigger than you, why would they pair you up?"

"Weights are applied to the cars to keep everyone at the same poundage. A couple of days before the race, there are practice runs. The cars and drivers are officially weighed then the cars are impounded so no one tries to add additional ballast."

They were silent the rest of the trip, each keeping their own counsel. When they approached the residential street where the race was to take place, a volunteer directed them to a parking lot used by a local car dealership to handle vehicle overflow. Cindi grabbed her backpack before exiting the car, and they walked around the corner. The street had been blocked off by a row of orange safety cones and wooden barriers.

"This looks great, just like a rural Le Mans," Preston said. Yellow caution tape had been tied to street signs and bales of hay lined the curbs, calling attention to the racing path. A portable stage doubled as a reviewing stand where the awards ceremony would be held. Black-and-white-checkered flags had been added to the roofline and fluttered in the early morning breeze. Gold and silver trophies stood straight and tall along the edge of the stage. The race wouldn't start for an hour and a half, but people had staked out the best viewing spots with their folding camp chairs. Food and souvenir vendors set up on the side streets, were doing a brisk business."

"I'm overwhelmed and impressed," Preston said, as his eyes traveled up the street to an open-sided white tent that designated the start of the race. "I see the cars are already lined up, but who gets to go first?"

"Every entrant fills out an application. Some chapters fan the paperwork facedown, and a member of the board selects the order of the racers. The All American Soap Box Derby has heat sheets that can be used."

"What time does the event officially start?"

"The opening ceremony is scheduled for eight-thirty, with the first cars starting off at nine. The Stock category, age's seven to ten, kicks off the race. Super stock, ages twelve to eighteen, goes next. The Masters is anyone to age twenty. There will be two car eliminations. After the first run, the kids are separated into winners and challengers and then regrouped. That's when things really heat up—eliminations, until there is only one winner in each category."

"Cindi Pearl, I'm floored by your knowledge of soap box derby racing. You mentioned the kids can be as old as twenty? They are a lot bigger than an eight-year-old."

"Nah, they use a few more milk cartons to make the car," Cindi laughed.

"Milk cartons?"

"The cars are made from recycled milk jugs. The kids in the Masters level actually lie flat, and only their helmets are visible. Two spotters wave checkered flags to let the kids know they reached the finish line. Observers tell the kids to brake, but many of them apply the brakes at the last minute and crash into the hay bales. It's foolish because they risk bending an axle. After their run, the kids make their way up the hill, and the cars are moved off the track by a volunteer manning a come-along dolly. The car is put on a flatbed trailer and brought to the start for the next round. That will be your assignment."

"Suppose one side of the street is faster than the other?"

"The cars switch sides the next time they come down. The official run is six hundred feet, and it takes approximately thirty seconds to run a race. The timers start the moment the kids leave the ramps."

"The committee has prepared for every contingency. Where will your brother be working? I look forward to meeting him."

"Unfortunately, he couldn't be here today. I mentioned Denny is a truck driver, and he's on his way to California. Come on. I'll sign you in, get us some shirts and introduce you around. Then we'll walk up the hill to the start of the race." Cindi paused and pressed the tips of her fingers to his forearm. His skin was already warm. "I'm sorry, Preston. At times my enthusiasm overpowers my brain. You didn't bring your cane, but if at any time your leg starts to bother you, just sit down. The local RV dealership brings in a travel trailer for us to use as our first aid station. Feel free to go inside and rest. It's air-conditioned."

"I appreciate your concern, but I purposely left my cane home. I've come to realize it's a psychological crutch. I no longer need it." He put a hand to her soft cheek. "Please don't worry. If my leg starts to bother me, I will rest."

Before he pulled his hand away, she deposited a kiss on the center of his palm. "Good enough. There are free drink and food stations for the kids and volunteers near the starting line. It's supposed to get up in the high eighties or low nineties, so make sure you have a bottle of water handy. Call my cell if you have any problems. I won't be far."

Before they parted, Preston put his hands to her shoulders and sampled the sweetness of her lips. He debated letting the kissing interest build up so he could enjoy more kisses, but he needed to taste her. "It's been a long time since someone was so concerned about my welfare," he said when he reluctantly released her mouth. "You've already pointed out the location of the Porta Johns, and I promise not to wander off. I've got my assignment."

"Let's go, Dolphin. You won't be shooting the curl, but you'll have the time of your life!"

They were interrupted half a dozen times by people wanting to say hello to Cindi before they got to the registration table to get their official shirts and name tags.

Preston adjusted the lanyard around his neck and watched volunteers line up the first six cars under the open-sided tent. Two others were placed on the starting ramps. "Every car has the sponsor's name painted on the side. What name do they put on the cars for the kids in foster care?"

"They actually came up with their own name. The A-Team."

"You mean like the old television show?"

"The story goes, the kids wanted the name because the A-Team was wrongly accused of a crime they didn't commit, but fought for the rights of the underdog."

"Sounds like a great bunch of kids. I noticed ten cars lined up against the fence on the other side of the first aid station. The seats are wider than the other others. Who are they for?"

Before she could tell him, the loudspeaker announced racers and handlers were to line up by their cars and stand by for the opening ceremonies.

"That's our cue," Cindi said hurriedly, grateful for the timely interruption. "I'll be on the reviewing stand, checking times, but I'll be back to help out with the Super Kids. You'd better hoof it down the hill."

With the reviewing stand in front of the finish line, Cindi had the advantage of keeping an eye on Preston. He worked well with the other men as they lifted each car onto the backs of the flatbed trailers. She neglected to mention he would be working with volunteers from the local high school ROTC. The six teenagers, dressed in gray military camo, fit the mold of the ideal fighting soldier.

Cindi didn't understand why the organizers had put the Super Kids toward the end of the first-round eliminations.

Another judge took over for her on the reviewing stand, and she followed the path to where the bales of hay ended and the cars were being loaded on the backs of the flatbeds. The time had come. She pasted a big smile on her face.

"Sorry, I need Preston to do another job."

"Miss Cindi, you can't take our strongest guy," protested Jason, one of the ROTC volunteers. "He's a former Army Ranger, a real hero."

"Don't worry. He'll be back for the finals."

Preston wiped the sweat from his brow with the sleeve of his shirt and then replaced his sunglasses over his eyes. "ROTC. Thanks for the warning. Those kids kept tossing questions at me while we worked. And no, I didn't claim to be a hero." He took the bottle of warm water out of his back pocket and killed his thirst. "To what do I owe the pleasure of your lovely company?"

Cindi figured he had to be tired and slowed her enthusiastic pace. "There is a special group of children I want you to meet, and they will be racing in about an hour. Let's make our way up the hill to the area alongside the first aid station."

He matched her footsteps and slipped a possessive arm about her waist. "You were right. I've really enjoyed myself. Some of those are kids are nuts. The guys are yelling 'brake, brake' and they plow right into the bales of hay."

"That's part of the fun." Cindi pressed a little closer to his side and savored these few private moments, despite the surrounding chaos. "Have you eaten?"

"No. Just drank a few bottles of water, as instructed." He winked and tightened his arm around her. "To be perfectly honest, I'm starving."

"We have time to get something before the next race."

After they devoured delicious Italian hot dogs, Cindi grabbed Preston's hand and led him toward the tent that had been erected to keep the sun off the children with special needs. "You've heard me mention the Super Kids. They have always been very special to me. The cars you noticed lined up by the fence have double seats, and handlers ride with each entrant. No matter where they place in the race, everyone is awarded a trophy just for being here."

A chorus of "Miss Cindi" became louder the closer she got to the tent. Three boys in wheelchairs rolled over to her. Jasper, the oldest of the boys, eyed Preston up and down.

"Who's the dude?"

"A friend," she smiled, ruffling his curly red hair. The fourteen-year-old had suffered from MS since he was born. Like all the other kids, he wore a blue-and-white derby shirt. The only difference was that the words "Super Kids" had been added under the derby car emblem.

Preston offered his hand in friendship. "The name is Preston, and I'm a very good friend. You seem to be the ringleader around here, so how about introducing me to your friends?"

Being designated the ringleader widened the smile on the boy's face, and he proceeded to introduce the other nine children. Two boys and three girls had Down syndrome. Trevor, an eight-year-old boy, had a degenerative disease that hindered his walking. Despite having both legs in braces and the need for crutches, all he did was smile. His dream was to play professional basketball.

The last person he met was an eleven-year-old girl. Belinda had covered her bald head with a pink baseball cap with the words "I beat cancer's butt." She was also in a wheelchair and missing the bottom half of her left leg.

Cindi was overwhelmed by Preston's acceptance of the Super Kids. He smiled, cajoled, and interacted in some way, with all of them. Someone had set up a portable basketball hoop, and the boys tossed a Nerf basketball between them. Preston joined right in and offered pointers. In the performance of an enthusiastic shot, Jasper accidently rolled his wheelchair into Preston's prosthetic leg.

His young face filled with remorse, and he immediately rolled back. "Hey, man, sorry. Hope I didn't hurt you."

The concern on the faces of all his young teammates cut right through Preston, and he found himself raising the bottom of his jeans to expose his prosthetic leg. "You didn't hurt me. I'm one of you."

Tears ran unheeded down Cindi's cheeks, and she wrapped her arms about her waist. Never had she loved him more.

Terry, one of the other advisors and Belinda's mother, approached Cindi and flipped a tissue in her direction. "Your boyfriend just gave them the greatest gift. If I wasn't married, I'd steal him from you." She'd just celebrated her fortieth birthday, but in her derby shirt and white shorts, her physical therapist body portrayed a woman in her late twenties.

"It isn't like that," Cindi said, wiping the wetness from her cheeks.

"You've got to be kidding. With that eye candy body, hunky face and great ass, jump his bones."

She sniffed and blew her nose. "It's not as if I haven't tried."

"Try harder, girl, try harder."

They'd just announced that the Super Kids' race would be starting in fifteen minutes. *Do it now, Cindi Pearl.* She walked up to Preston, slipped her arm about his waist and addressed all the kids. "I need everyone to hydrate and then settle down."

He tossed the Nerf ball in his hand to Jasper, accepted the bottle of water from Cindi and drank it down. "Thanks. They can move in those wheelchairs."

"That was a pretty wonderful thing you did for those kids. You just raised yourself to hero status in their eyes."

"From you, I'll take that as a compliment, but I only wanted to show them anything is possible. And stop using that word."

"Okay! Okay! I need a favor," she blurted.

"Why am I not surprised?" He grinned. "What is it?"

"I need you to ride in Jasper's car as a handler."

Before Preston could answer, a family walked into the tent and approached Terry and Belinda with big smiles. Terry's brother apologized for being late. His wife was obviously pregnant, and he carried their two-year-old little boy in his right arm.

The air about Cindi suddenly chilled, and she didn't have to touch Preston to sense a change in his mood. His eyes were riveted on the man holding the child.

Preston stared at the man dressed in a white T-shirt and knee-length shorts. The man seemed unconcerned that his prosthetic leg was exposed to inquisitive eyes. His left arm was missing from the elbow down. When his wife leaned in to him with an affectionate hug, he kissed her on the cheek then kissed his little boy. They were a unit—a happy, loving family.

Cindi was frightened by the panic-stricken look in Preston's eyes, and she wrapped her hand around his stiffened arm. "Are you okay?"

A vise of uncertainty seized his entire body. It was happening again, just like the night of the Fourth of July ceremony. He'd come face to face with another turning point in his life. He didn't feel sick, but his heart was beating out of control and sweat ran down his shoulder blades. He stepped back, making her hand fall away. "No, I can't," he choked out. "I have to get out of here."

She turned her head and followed his gaze. Not seeing anything unusual, only the young family talking with Terry, she turned back to Preston. "What's wrong? What do you mean you can't?" Her questions were useless.

He was gone.

CHAPTER 10

Cindi slammed into the quiet kitchen and threw her backpack on the table. There wasn't a word in any language to describe the intensity of her anger. That jerk just left! Got in his goddamn three-hundred-thousand-dollar car and drove off, but not before he walked away uttering "I can't." One request, one simple request: ride with a Super Kid. It was okay to lead them on, let them think he was their friend, "Oh, I'm one of you," and then he runs off with his tail between his legs. Heartless son of a bitch!

The rat fink's fancy car was in the driveway. It was time to have it out with him, once and for all. She stormed out of the house, hurried up the barn ramp and took the iron steps to the loft two at a time. She stopped at the top of the stairs to catch her breath. The bird in the clock chose that moment to cuckoo six times. "Oh, shut up, you wooden bird brain," she snarled as her eyes fell upon the table. She noticed a lined yellow pad and pen. "Probably writing me a dear Jane letter." The thought stabbed her in the heart. Woman's curiosity drew her to read the handwritten note.

Cindi, I'm a shit, a big, dumb, heartless shit. I ran off like a spineless coward and left you and the kids hanging. I don't deserve you, but I can't help loving you. I want to confess my love, but it wouldn't be right. I shouldn't have let myself fall in love with you. Maybe it's time we cooled off...

The message stopped.

"No! No! You can't stop here!" Cindi picked up the note with trembling hands and re-read what he'd written. *In love with you* were the only words of importance in the stupid confession. Preston loved her!

The sound of running water drew her attention to the bathroom. As the saying went, you could lead a horse to water, but you couldn't make him drink. What more could she do to make him see he was a hot, sexy stud, capable of making love as well as the next guy? She didn't want the next guy. She wanted him. The big, dumb, heartless shit loved her!

"Here goes nothing." She grabbed the bottom of her T-shirt, pulled it through the neck and tugged it down, exposing a bit of cleavage and bared stomach. The word *no* wasn't in her vocabulary. "PJ, fire up your jackhammer!" At the last minute, she kicked off her sneakers.

Her footsteps slowed the closer she got to the bathroom. Go in like gangbusters or take things a little slower? Sure, he'd confessed his love, but wanting to make love to her was his decision, not hers. How could he claim to love her and then suggest they cool things off? She was more confused than ever. She also needed an explanation as to why he'd run off. It was time to lay all her cards on the table and confront him.

The bathroom door was open, and his naked form was a shivery shadow beyond the wall of frosted glass blocks. A cloud of moisture drifted around the ceiling, and his soap gave off a woodsy scent. She stopped at the wide opening and silently gasped at his muscular back and firm buttocks suffering the hammering spray from four different shower heads. He ignored the built-in seat and gripped the special metal shower bars. It was obvious he hadn't neglected the gym since his injury. His entire body was strong, tight, and sturdy. His delicious ass was so firm she wanted to sink her teeth into his flesh. Her breath caught when he shifted his hands to a second bar and turned around. His eyes were closed and he appeared to be pondering a problem while standing under the buffeting shower.

A few moments later, he sensed her presence, and his eyes flew open. She leaned a hip against a column of glass blocks and went on the defensive.

"You left me! You goddamn left me at the derby." Her voice echoed off the walls of the enclosure. "I had to make some cockamamie excuse to the kids that you had an emergency. They all said you were cool, a real hero, but I told them you were a selfish asshole." She waved the yellow sheet from the pad. "Got your message. Changed your mind about loving me and want to cool things off, just like that." She paused to let her eyes appreciate his well-toned body, stopping at his groin. He was so gorgeous, so well-endowed, that she swallowed hard. In the past few moments, he'd gone from parade rest to attention.

Preston never anticipated her seeing what he'd written down while coming to a life-changing decision, or expected her to walk into his shower. Then again, this was a determined Cindi Pearl.

He remained standing and gripped the support bar more tightly. "Do we have to discuss this while I'm naked in the shower?"

"Yes! That's your forte. Run off without an explanation!"

"I guess I deserved that." He sighed. "I didn't mean for you to see that note. They were my private thoughts." *She hasn't looked at my leg*, his mind cried, once, twice.

"You had to write it down and practice how to dump me! I agree with your statement. You are a shit. I've done everything humanly possible to make you feel like a man, even jumping into the guppy-filled pond half-naked. All you did was laugh and offer me your damn shirt! I get more affection from my pygmy goat! I'm not beautiful enough for you!"

He was exactly what she described, a selfish shit. From the moment he'd left the race, his mind had clamored with indecision. His long road to recovery had been fraught with many personal challenges, some of them painful, but the next turning point was the most important one he had to face. He'd been wrong, in so many ways. He'd denied them both, but no more. His prolonged dry spell was about to end, with only one woman, his Cindi Pearl. *She's seen me and hasn't run off. Will she be able to touch me?* "I can't hear all of your insults. Come closer."

She gave no mind to the hail of water and stepped inside the enclosure. "I'm not beautiful enough for you!" she shouted.

Little bit more, he silently noted, getting ready to change the angle of the top nozzle. "No, you're not beautiful."

Her eyes widened, and she took exception to the insult. Determined footsteps brought her closer. She didn't expect to get pummeled in the face with a stream of warm water. "You rat," she sputtered, spitting water out of her mouth.

Her objection was half-hearted when busy hands tugged her wet T-shirt over her head and unhooked the front of her lacy orchid bra. "Who gave you permission to remove my clothes?"

"You did," he laughed, "the moment you invaded my shower."

She tugged off her soaking wet shorts and bikinis. "Why?"

"Because I want you naked so I can see your magnificent body." He didn't bother with niceties and used one hand to toss her sopping wet clothes outside the shower.

"Wrong answer." Her body was totally exposed to him, but she didn't feel the least bit uncomfortable or shy.

"Because I am so goddamn horny, my mind is consumed with making love to you every waking moment of the day." He took her hand and wrapped her fingers around the throbbing proof of his confession. "This is what you do to me." When her silky skin met with his flesh, he forced himself not to move. Sheer pleasure filled his body when her fingers tightened around him.

Instant heat singed her flesh. When he slowly lowered his eyelids, she felt him shudder with pleasure. Her fingers had a mind of their own and started to explore the smooth flesh that surrounded his steel-like strength. Two hands wouldn't be enough to capture his hard length. She wanted to look down at her hand, but guilt and deceit forced her to release him. "This is wrong. I shouldn't be here." Cindi lowered her head and turned away, but a band of strength encircled her waist. Water cascaded on her head and streamed down her cheeks, camouflaging her tears. "I came here under false pretenses."

"Bullshit! Don't go anywhere." Two inches of water covered the bottom of the shower. "I'm going to turn the water off before we drown."

Preston lowered his body to the tile floor and drew her down with him. He wanted nothing more than to get her into bed, but his Cindi needed to apologize, for something. *She still hasn't paid any attention to my leg.*

"Okay, tell me," he coaxed.

She focused on the whirlpool of water circling the drain. "When I read your note—and by the way, I love you too—I was going to try to seduce you, but I realized that was wrong. I can't force you to make love with me. That is a decision you have to make on your own."

Preston didn't think his heart could withstand another blow, and he drew her closer to straddle his lap. It took every part of his being not to thrust into her. "You love me?"

"Do you think I would have gone through all this if I didn't love you?" She pressed her wet forehead to his. "I wouldn't care if you had two heads."

"That's good to know." The hard tips of her breasts branded his chest, and nothing had ever felt more wonderful. Before he made love to her, though, they needed to resolve another problem. "You had another reason for invading my shower."

"Why did you leave the derby so abruptly? Was it because I asked you to ride with Jasper?"

Preston shook his head and pushed a clump of wet hair away from her face. "Wow, I wasn't expecting that. Guess I have been pretty bad. You actually think I was disturbed by the sight of those wonderful kids who live life to the fullest?"

"What else was I supposed to think? You said, 'I can't.'"

"Yes, I said that, but it wasn't the Super Kids. They are all great. It was Belinda's uncle who showed up right before the Super Kids' race. He has a prosthetic leg, half his left arm is missing and he wasn't wearing long pants."

Cindi tried to ignore the throbbing length that found a home in her groin. She ached to enfold him in her hand but forced herself to concentrate on what he was saying. "That's it?"

"No! He held a two-year-old in his arm, and his wife was very pregnant. Both were laughing and smiling. They were a family."

"So, you want a baby?"

"No! Not yet, anyway. Don't you get it? Saying 'I can't' referred to my fear that I couldn't make love. I've been wallowing in a hell of self-pity, avoiding relationships and having sex, because I thought the sight of my missing leg would turn a woman off. My goddamn pride has stopped me from wearing shorts. I go swimming when I'm totally alone." He brought her tight against him and he groaned when the fold in her leg cradled him like a baby in its mother's arm. *Home sweet home, almost*, he thought. "I've been such an idiot."

"I agree, but I figured that out for myself. Why do you think I've been throwing myself at you?" She'd never been hotter in her life. It felt like a fire stick was lodged in her groin.

"It was working, believe me." He inhaled deeply. "Any more questions?" He ached with need and didn't know how much longer he could suffer through all this small talk.

"Last one. Does this mean we are going to have sex?" When he didn't immediately respond, she tipped her head to the side. "Don't tell me you have to give it more thought."

"We are not going to have sex."

"We're not!"

He gathered her wet face in his hands and sampled the wetness on her delectable mouth. "We, my darling Cindi Pearl, are going to make love. It will be a first, because I've never made love with part of my leg missing."

"Hallelujah!" she cheered. "Neither have I, so it will be a first for both of us."

Preston's hearty laugh echoed off the shower walls.

She stood up first and passed him his crutch that he'd set in the corner of the shower, like it was an everyday occurrence, and grabbed two bath towels off the bathroom rack. "Meet you in bed," she teased, fluffing the towel across her wet hair, trying not to make this moment more awkward than necessary.

Cindi stepped into the bedroom wrapped in her towel and stopped. "How come you didn't mention the three amigos have taken a liking to your bed?" Donut was sprawled between Cupcake and Muffin.

"They were on my bed yesterday when I got home from work. That's why I covered the comforter with the old sheet." Preston hadn't bothered with a towel and lowered his lips to her warm shoulder. "Let's say we evict them."

"Good idea. You make yourself comfortable and I'll convince them the ugly orange couch is much softer." They were both stalling, and she didn't know who was more nervous.

"Good luck." Preston moved to the side of the bed, sat down and lowered his crutch to the floor. He swung his legs up, debating whether or not to crawl under the quilt. His heart was racing from anticipation. *Stop. You're acting like a teenage boy who is about to make love for the first time. This is Cindi, your love. It's going to be beautiful, mind-blowing. She won't run off.*

"Our chaperones didn't like the couch and left." Cindi whipped off the towel and threw it on the chair in the corner. She climbed on the mattress and moved stealthily across the bed on all fours. "Ready or not, here I come." He was magnificently splayed against a stack of pillows with his legs slightly spread, inviting her to appreciate his readiness to make love. "PJ, there's no turning back. From the look of your jackhammer, you are raring to go." Inside, she was burning up from the want of this man, but she had to do this right so they both enjoyed their first special time together.

"I'm so ready for you. No more teasing." He opened his arms in invitation. "Come here, minx. Straddle my lap."

Her palms were sweating when she linked their fingers. "We are in this together. Remember, I love you." She swung her leg over his hips and wrapped her fingers around his throbbing hardness. With infinite care, she slowly lowered herself on his hot, thick length and brought him home. She hadn't made love with anyone in a long time, and she gently rotated her hips to adjust to his large size. Then he was completely inside. They were one. Her eyelids fluttered closed and she wallowed in the sexy realm of heat meeting heat. He was hers, finally.

The hand that guided him into her body was the key to open the dam of trepidation he'd kept back for seven years.

Incredible sensations exploded throughout every part of his body and awakened dormant nerve endings. The moment he was inside, he moaned from the stunning reality that he was fully joined with the woman he loved, his Cindi Pearl.

At his groan, her eyes flew open, wondering if she'd done something wrong. His eyes were closed and he appeared to be frozen in time. His hands still gripped her hips. "Are you in pain?"

A single tear slid down his cheek, and he opened his eyes to gaze upon the angel who'd erased one of his deepest fears. "You took me by surprise."

She leaned forward and planted nibbling kisses on his lips. "Did I screw up?"

"No, my love, you screwed down. I've never felt anything more incredible or healing. I love being inside you, but I've really got to move because I'm about to explode. Tell me you are on the pill because I'm not wearing any body armor."

"I'm protected." She wiggled her hips, and if possible, he seemed to swell inside her. "You haven't kissed me once, so would you mind correcting that error?"

He claimed her mouth with a consuming kiss, and started to move, slowly at first, not wanting to hurt her. His Cindi, his beautiful love, accepted everything he gave. Their moans of pleasure blended with each smooth plunge. When he couldn't hold back anymore, he quickened his strokes and released years of pent-up denial and longing.

Moonlight painted the naked bodies of the entwined lovers. Neither had given a thought to the passage of time as they created a paradise of their own making.

"I love you, Cindi Pearl. My heart is so full of love for you, it could burst." He tightened his arm about her shoulder and played with the silky strands of her hair brushing her shoulder. "How come you didn't look at my leg when you first saw me in the shower?"

"It wasn't a priority. You said you loved me in one sentence and then suggested we cool it in another."

"I'm sorry you misunderstood. I meant we should cool our hot bodies in the pond."

"It's a lame excuse, but an acceptable explanation."

"Did you really tell the kids I was a selfish asshole?"

"No," she laughed. "I said you had an emergency. Terry and Belinda brought me home." Cindi was quiet for a troubled moment and let her eyes travel down his shortened leg. "Does it hurt?"

He cautioned himself not to panic when he saw where she focused her attention. "Not now. Sometimes, when I push myself too hard, it gets a little sore. Why?"

She sat up and traced his chin with her finger. "Can I touch your leg?"

Once again, she took him by surprise. She was amazing. "Why?"

"I'm curious."

"Just don't run out of here with the screaming memes because it's disgusting."

"Don't be ridiculous. It's part of you."

"I'll understand if you change your mind." He padded the back of his head with his hands and spread his legs a little more, offering himself up to inspection. *It's okay, it's going to be okay*, he told himself. "I'm all yours."

"You certainly are." Cindi knelt at the bottom of the bed and lovingly caressed the stump with the tips of her fingers. "It's hard, yet soft and so strong. I can't imagine what you went through."

"Your fingers feel like velvet against my skin," he said with a sigh of pleasure, before sharing his private thoughts. "It wasn't so much the physical pain, but emotional. When it first happened, a person's first instinct is survival, followed by the shock of losing a part of your body. In bed, especially at night, your mind explodes with all the things you won't be able to do. For me, it was from surfing, skiing and running right down to getting up in the middle of the night and walking to the bathroom. My right foot was gone, so how would I be able to drive a car? A friend of mine lost both legs, and he joked we would be saving money on shoes. The psychologists and physical therapists were great. Everyone assured me I would have my life back as soon as I got the prosthesis. I didn't think so at the time, but they were right." He lifted his head slightly to enjoy her irresistible body. Her delectable upturned breasts had tasted delicious and he was eager to sample more, a great deal more. "Other than medical personnel, you are the only person to touch me."

Cindi continued to lovingly caress the rounded tip. "What gave you the idea you wouldn't be able to make love? Another falsity," she added with a grin.

"It was just after I started physical therapy with my artificial limb. A guy's wife came in to visit while he was working out. An adjustment was needed, so they had to remove his prosthesis. They wanted her to be familiar with the removal and encouraged her to help. Once it was removed, she stared in horror at her husband's injury and ran out, saying she couldn't bear to touch the ugly limb."

"She was a cruel bitch."

"I was too happy learning how to walk with my new leg to give it too much thought. When it happened a few more times, the experience planted a grim seed in my brain. What woman would want to look at or touch me, with or without my prosthesis?"

"You are beautiful, all of you."

When she lowered her head and brushed his skin with her lips, his heart soared. Her heartfelt giving was the most wonderful thing he'd ever felt. "I'd go through every pain-filled horror again if I knew it would bring me to you."

Tears rushed down her cheeks, and she wiped them away with the corner of the sheet. The tightness in her chest was from the love she had for this very special man. She crawled on all fours and threw herself against his chest.

"Don't ever think you aren't capable of physically satisfying me. The second and third time, you were on top, and from the look of your jackhammer, you are primed and ready for round four."

"I have a lot of years to make up for." He grinned and rolled on top of her.

Sunday morning, Cindi invited him to go to church and then breakfast at the Spoonful. The place was packed, as usual, and they were lucky to be seated in a booth without too long a wait.

Sallie Mae passed them red leather-bound menus and sensed a change in two of her favorite people, especially Preston Reynolds. He appeared more relaxed, comfortable with himself. Then a light bulb of understanding went on in her head. She bent down and whispered something in Preston's ear before announcing the day's specials.

He winked and gave her a thumbs-up.

"Tell me she didn't just ask if we've had sex?" Cindi questioned in a hurried whisper behind her menu.

"Okay, I won't tell you that."

"It's a wonder she didn't ask how many times."

"Six." He winked before holding the menu in front of his grinning face. He felt like a million dollars. No, make it a trillion dollars. Who knew that making love on a wooden dock, watching the sun rise, could be so exhilarating and satisfying? The swim that followed had topped off their welcome of the new day. It blew his mind when Cindi helped him remove his device and protective sleeve. They were soon joined by Cupcake and Muffin. Donut had stretched out on their towels. Preston was inclined to jump in the air and click his heels, but that was something he wasn't quite capable of doing. Maybe someday.

They gave their orders to the waitress and sampled some of the Danish pastries on the table, prepared by Samantha. There would be no need to advertise her new shop. Word of mouth was already spreading the news about her delicious baked goods.

"What would you like to do today?" Cindi asked before sipping her orange juice.

All he did was grin.

"Women of the world, beware. PJ Reynolds is back in the saddle."

"I beg to differ with you, Cindi Pearl. There is only one woman who will man the reins on this stud."

Cindi shook her head and leaned over the red Formica-topped table. "We are nuts, absolutely nuts. This conversation is ridiculous."

A very satisfied gleam filled his eyes. "Speak for yourself. Cindi Pearl, I haven't been this happy in a long time."

"Me either." She had delicious aches in her body, ones she would gladly suffer for a lifetime.

"Okay, what is the second or third thing you would like to do today?" She captured his hand and linked their fingers. "Seriously."

"I'd like to take a ride to the closest mall and check out a couple of men's stores. I could use a few pairs of shorts. When we get back, maybe we can take care of my first priority."

"Deal." She blushed. She really could use a nap. Sleep had been the last thing on both their minds during the night.

They were just about to leave when Cindi noticed a couple approaching the booth. The older woman looked a great deal better than she had the last time they'd sat at a board of directors' meeting of the soap box derby organization.

"Cindi Pearl, I thought that was you."

"Mildred, how are you? You are looking well." Cindi had always wondered how the woman could see out of her Coke-bottle-thick glasses. She favored loose, flowery dresses and a thick application of makeup to appear years younger than her early sixties. Her black hair was caught in a neat bun atop her head, but the white streak following her hairline reminded Cindi of the bride of Frankenstein.

"The bypass operation was successful, but my physical activities are still low-key. I won't be able to get involved with the soap box derby again for quite a while."

"I'm glad everything worked out. Mildred Cummings, I'd like you to meet Preston Reynolds. We work together at Adams Security, and he's helping me reconcile the soap box derby accounts." She kept it to herself that there was a great deal of money missing. Cindi caught the way Mildred's back stiffened the moment she mentioned the derby accounts.

"There shouldn't be any problems," she quickly stated. "I took over for my husband and have kept the financial records for ten years. I've been an accountant for thirty-five years, and my end-of-the-year balance sheets were perfect." Mildred put a hand to her chest, drawing attention to various gold-and-diamond rings on her fingers. "Pardon my manners. This is my son, Harold. He's been by my side through this terrible ordeal."

Preston acknowledged the introduction with a nod, but never held out the hand he'd tightened into a fist. He already knew the man to be single and thirty-nine. He drove a garbage truck for a living. They'd just been formally introduced to the person who dumped the bags of garbage in the barn and kidnapped Donut, Cupcake and Muffin. Preston was tempted to punch the guy in the mouth for the insults he'd spray-painted on Cindi's car, but that would only reveal the ongoing investigation. The bastard's time would come.

CHAPTER 11

After running into the two people Preston knew to be the cause of Cindi's problems, he decided to bring everyone up to date on his findings. He'd spoken with their boss the previous evening, and Lincoln confirmed he would be available Monday morning and would invite Jessie as an official police presence.

Cindi sat at the conference table in Lincoln's office and nursed her mug of much-needed coffee, hoping the caffeine would hurry up and do its job. She avoided eye contact with the sexy stud who had kept her up half the night. He had more stamina than a real construction jackhammer. She'd had no intentions of spending the night in his bed, but he was so damn hard to resist. This morning he was dressed in dark gray tailored trousers and a lighter gray shirt. Why did he have to choose that particular rose-striped tie to wear this morning? She yawned and patted a polite hand in front of her mouth. "Sorry, didn't get much sleep last night."

"It must have been the thunder and lightning," Jessie remarked and smiled when her husband set a cup of coffee on the table in front of her. "It woke up the entire house. Edie came into our room to announce we were not to be scared because the angels were bowling." Jessie adjusted the belt on her uniform trousers. At the rate she was expanding, she would have to switch to maternity clothes in the next few weeks.

"It wasn't the kettle drums of Mother Nature," Cindi grumbled and sipped more coffee.

Jessie caught her statement and fluttered her eyelashes in a way that said *hubba-hubba.*

"Love is in the air," Linc said, taking a seat next to his wife.

Preston wasn't the least bit embarrassed they knew he'd made love to Cindi. Nothing could dampen his happiness. He took a seat at the table next to his love and forced himself not to touch her. The soft pink of her blouse reminded him of the wild mountain laurel bordering the pond. Last evening, after cooling off in the tepid water, they'd stretched out on the dock. He'd feathered the tip of her beautiful breast with a delicate flower and savored the hardened crown with his mouth. Then he nipped his way down the center of her body and sampled the delicious sweetness between her legs. He was out of his mind in love with her. A yawn accidently escaped.

"Insomnia must be contagious. It's almost an epidemic at our house," Linc said with a little chuckle and received a kick under the table from his blushing wife.

"No comment." Preston winked at Cindi and booted up his laptop. "Okay, down to business. I'll begin with the theft of the funds." A PowerPoint presentation appeared on one of the wall screens. "Mildred Cummings was very clever and I really had to dig. It has gone on longer than one event. She used the accounts as her own bank, withdrawing and returning funds within the same year. Getting sick threw a monkey wrench into the works."

His love was sure to get upset by his next statement, so he addressed Lincoln and Jessie directly. "If anyone other than me had investigated the records, Lieutenant Adams would be escorting Cindi out of the building in handcuffs for embezzlement. The records show that Cindi Pearl Sullivan withdrew the money and forged the signature of the president of the board of directors."

"What! The tiredness in Cindi's body was consumed by outrage. "I did no such thing! That old coot with the bride of Frankenstein hair is an embezzling bitch! When we met her at the café yesterday, she was positive all of the accounts would balance."

"Bride of Frankenstein?" Jessie interrupted, not expecting an answer.

"Everything is in perfect order. Your name is on the account to sign for and administer payment of expenses," Preston explained. "You aren't the first one she's used as a scapegoat. I found other names that were eliminated after she returned various amounts of money. She didn't expect us to go way back and discover her money game. Mildred actually picked up where her deceased husband left off."

"What is she spending the money on?" Jessie asked.

"She had a gambling problem. I did a few deep searches, and it appears she's gotten it under control." He patted the back of Cindi's hand. "Your bride of Frankenstein isn't a total monster. She's been taking in foster children over the years, but three chose to stay when they turned eighteen. We met one of them yesterday, Harold Webber. He drives a garbage truck."

"That's the first piece to fall into place," Lincoln said. "After you called the other night, I had our techs review the data from the retail store at the camp. There were only six cash purchases of the little goat." Lincoln slid several eight-by-ten pictures across the table. "Anyone look familiar?"

"Harold was a busy man," Cindi said, tapping the color picture of the garbage man. "I wonder why Mildred never told us she took in foster children."

"People keep secrets for different reasons." Preston avoided direct eye contact with Cindi. He was walking a thin line in the secret department.

"Now Reggie's e-mail makes sense," Preston said. "I had our guy in New York trace the package. The company has no record of an order being sent to Cindi Pearl Sullivan at this address. Harold purchased the stuffed animal and must have dropped it off at our mailroom himself."

Jessie looked at her husband. "You should be able to check your own security records."

"Will do, as soon as we finish our meeting, Lieutenant Taylor-Adams."

"We know how he got the garbage and when he purchased the stuffed animal. That should be enough for the police to pick him up for questioning," Cindi said.

"You are right, and the charges might stick. Before we go any further, let me tell you about the other two people who live in Mildred's house. Ron Tremont and Carole Gibbons. She took them in when they were seven years old. Both are physically challenged and can't work outside the home. Carole is thirty-three and is wheelchair-bound. She's an artist, and her dream is to have a showing at a gallery. Ron is also thirty-three and confined to a wheelchair. He is tech-savvy and tests new computer games, but he wants to design his own games. Harold pays a live-in aide to take care of them. Carole and Ron get a small amount from Social Security, but it isn't enough. Mildred is sixty-two, and her insurance plan didn't cover all of her medical expenses. Over the years, she's provided special schooling and professional tutoring so her kids could pursue their interests in art and computers. She couldn't have done more for them if they were her own natural-born children."

"How did you find out about their hopes and dreams?" Cindi asked.

"During my research into Mildred's financial background, I noticed the name of a physical therapist that comes to the house twice a week. I reached out to the therapist I worked with and asked if he could get me any information without violating patient confidentiality."

"She could get a lot of money if she sold those diamond-and-ruby rings she wears."

"Sorry to burst your bubble, sweetheart, but the stones aren't real." Calling her *sweetheart* in front of Lincoln and Jessie came as natural as breathing.

"In other words, if we arrest Harold and Mildred, the other two will be left high and dry," Jessie said.

"That's about the size of it." Preston foresaw the dilemma Cindi would have to face, but refrained from offering his opinion. The decision to prosecute would have to be hers.

"Harold threatened to harm Donut, ruined Pansy, dumped rotten, smelly garbage on our property and scared the life out of me by kidnapping our animals! What about the money Mildred embezzled? We've started an official investigation, and my name is on those records. I can still be arrested!"

"No one is going to arrest you," Jessie assured her.

"When you look at the total picture, and I'm not saying he shouldn't pay for what he did, but Harold's motives weren't selfish," Lincoln said. "He wanted to protect his family and foster mother because he knew she had embezzled the funds. Who knows—if she hadn't gotten sick, she might have put the money back like she did the other times."

"I can talk to the judge and fill her in on the situation," Jessie offered. "You know my mother will take into consideration all phases of the investigation. She can devise a way to make them pay, but you'll have to work with her since all of the complaints are in your name."

Cindi eyed the others sitting at the table and shook her head at the irony of the situation. "I know what you are all thinking. Life just isn't fair!" She exhaled a deep sigh. "Guess it's time to fall back on my personal motto, 'Do a good deed, for a friend in need.'"

CHAPTER 12

That afternoon, the three amigos were in a snit. They'd gathered on top of Preston's bed, their new favorite meeting place. Since their host was well aware of their gathering spot, he'd covered the bed with an older, softer blanket.

A new animal had been brought to the farm. A girl, a prissy pygmy donkey Preston bought for Cindi. She sashayed up to each of them, sniffed and turned a conceited tail. Miss Samantha fawned over the little animal and called her Cheesecake. Said she needed a pretty straw bonnet with yellow-and-white daisies. The amigos decided to boycott the little critter and sulk.

Preston pulled down the drive and parked along side the barn. He was glad to be home. He'd been given two new projects and asked himself why people had to be so dishonest. Depending on what he'd found, a trip to their LA office might be in his future.

An hour after their morning meeting, Jessie called. The judge agreed to meet with Cindi tomorrow morning to discuss the complaints. She asked Preston to join them and bring along all of the evidence he'd gathered on the mother and son.

He was anxious to get home before Cindi and wanted to see her reaction to the new addition to their farm family. He took off his tie and unbuttoned his shirt on his way into the bedroom and stopped short at the sight of his welcoming committee. They didn't move off their spot on the bed, but gave him the evil eye.

"Don't tell me. You three are jealous of the new kid around here," Preston laughed, tossing his clothes in the hamper. "This place is new to her, and she could use a few friends. How would you three feel if you went to a new home and were snubbed by the locals?" He lifted Donut into his arm and played the guilt card. "I'm surprised at you. She's a pygmy too. That must mean she's some kind of relative or something." When the goat licked him on the cheek, Preston figured his message had gotten across. "I'm going back downstairs to wait for Cindi Pearl to meet Cheesecake. Stay here and sulk if you want." He pulled his black muscle shirt over his head, stepped into his knee-length jean shorts and reflected on the past few minutes. He'd just had a one-sided conversation with three animals. It was crazy, but he liked the new life's path he'd chosen to follow, as long he walked that trail with Cindi.

"Do a good deed, for a friend in need." Cindi had muttered the phrase half a dozen times as she drove home from work. It stuck in her craw that she would most likely drop the complaints. Carole and Ron would suffer if she didn't do the right thing. There had to be a way to make Mildred and Harold pay, especially Harold. Her heart went out to Carole and Ron, wishing there was a way to help them fulfill their dreams.

The sight of Preston's fancy car brought a smile to her face. She could use some cheering up. One or two of his kisses would do the job. When she parked Sam's Jeep in the equipment shed, she glanced at the adjoining empty space. She missed her little car. She hoped the shop would have Pansy fully restored the following week. The insurance company had sent her a check, minus her deductible. She was out five hundred dollars because of that horse's ass, Harold!

Something was different when she headed for the house. The three amigos hadn't come out to greet her. Then she heard laughter in the rear of the barn. She changed direction and headed for the cow paddock. Preston and Samantha were perched on the top rail of the post-and-rod fence surrounding the pen, watching the animals frolic to a silent tune. Her eyes widened at the new addition to their farm.

The pygmy donkey had to be a girl with her cute bonnet. Cupcake, Muffin and Donut marched single file around the pewter-gray donkey. Pound Cake and Brownie retreated to a corner of the compound to watch the show. Cookie perched atop a fence post and heralded the newcomer with numerous a cock-a-doodle-dos.

Cindi was at a loss for words. The small ass had been fitted with a peg at the knuckle of the rear right leg. The previous owner had wrapped tape around her fake leg in a rainbow of colors.

Preston heard the sniffles behind him, and he hopped down from the fence. He wasn't surprised at the tears running down his love's cheeks. "How do you like the new addition to our family?"

The words "our family" zeroed in on her heart, and she threw her arms around his waist. "I love her! What's her name? Where did she come from?" Preston tenderly dabbed at the wetness on Cindi's cheeks with a white handkerchief.

Sam's heart clutched at the sight of the embracing couple. Being alone had never been a problem for her until these two had shown her that real love just might be possible. Only one man had ever come close to cracking the shell of hardness around her heart, but she had been on an undercover assignment and didn't even know his real name.

"You are not going to believe it," Samantha said, "but her previous owner called her Cheesecake."

"Perfect!"

"I came across a picture of the little donkey while doing research," Preston explained. "A local number was provided. Cheesecake has been the town vet's patient all along, so Lisa Kay made the arrangements." Preston wiggled his brows. "I just want to make a slight change to her name and call her Cherry Cheesecake."

"Cherry?" Cindi laughed, hoping she wasn't blushing. She slipped a casual arm around Preston's waist and slid a hand into the back pocket of his new shorts. The sleeveless shirt defined the raised slope of muscles on the upper part of his arms and heated up her libido. He was so built and deserved a pinch on his fine ass for adding the name Cherry to their new pet's name. No, she'd just bite it later.

Things were heating up fast, and Sam decided to make an exit. She jumped down from the rail and paused next to the embracing pair. "You'll find a tray of bruschetta and fresh mozzarella and a bottle of wine chilling in the refrigerator. Dinner is in the oven. Dessert is cherry cheesecake." Sam winked.

"Aren't you going to join us?" Cindi asked.

"Nope. I've got a date."

"With a man?" Cindi asked. Sam never dated.

"Yes, but it's not what you think. I'm meeting Sam Morlock at Tea in Time to go over blueprints. Marie Kelly's twins, Connor and Brandon, have agreed to install the heating and air conditioning at a reduced rate and take care of all the special electrical wiring. If you two decide to go skinny dipping, watch out—I'll be back by eleven," Sam called out with a laugh on her way to the house.

Samantha had set the table on the porch and lighted candles under three glass chimneys. The flickering firelight invited moths to dance in the soft radiance. The setting sun painted the sky a peachy-orange hue before fading into a soft bluish-gray, a prelude to the velvet darkness. It was a perfect night for lovers.

"If Samantha ever decided to open a restaurant, there would be a stampede," Preston said, wiping his mouth with a blue linen napkin. "That is the best eggplant parmesan I've ever eaten."

Cindi leaned back in her white wicker chair and put a hand to her full stomach. "She knows it's my favorite. Cooking is just a hobby and a job. Baking is her passion."

"I know you've worked with her for ten years, a lot longer than I have, but do you know why she doesn't date? She's a very beautiful woman."

"She's never gone into great detail about her life before she started working for Lincoln. I do know she ran away from home when she was sixteen and waitressed in a truck stop. She met and married an asshole trucker when she was eighteen. Their so-not-wedded-bliss lasted six months because he couldn't keep his dick in his pants. He and his latest bimbo were killed in a motorcycle accident. Sam pulled her life together, went to college and became one of Adams Security's first undercover operatives. She's the best, and Lincoln was sorry she resigned. Opening Tea in Time has been her dream. She occasionally freelances for Lincoln to bring in extra money."

"Any man would be lucky to have her."

When Cindi started to gather their dirty dishes, Preston helped. "Let's clean up and head to our favorite spot." He had a little surprise. Since they spent so much time by the water, he'd made a slight improvement to the setting.

They brought their glasses and what was left in the bottle of wine to the pond. To her delight, he'd added low solar-powered lamps around the shoreline and bench for soft lighting. The ducks were in the water, along with their guest mallards. Cherry and Donut sprawled on the dock. The tops of their heads were brushing.

Cindi snuggled on Preston's lap and leaned her head into his shoulder. "Tell me the truth. Who did you buy Cherry for, you or me?"

He tightened his arms and kissed the top of her head. Her hair had the scent of sweet peaches. "I've been waiting for you to ask that question, and to be perfectly honest, I don't know. An article on rescue animals came up while I was working on a project. I clicked on it and there was Cheesecake. Nicola Harding, her owner, accepted an assignment in London and was looking for responsible caregivers. I called Lisa Kay and she put it all together. If you really need an answer to your question, the little donkey is a gift of my love for you."

"That is very beautiful, but Cheesecake is a great deal more." Cindi sat up and cupped his chin in her hands. He'd started wearing contacts and she missed his sexy, nerdy glasses. "Cherry Cheesecake is a symbol of acceptance, your acceptance of who and what you are: healed and complete. I love you, Preston Reynolds. I wake up every day and can't wait to see you smile, hear your wonderful laugh, kiss you. Together we make up a whole."

Preston was awestruck by the boundless depth of her love and leaned in to give her a deep, enduring kiss. "It's taken a while for me to accept what you've known all along. You helped me acknowledge I might have been some kind of hero. I look forward to surfing and water-skiing. You make me laugh, I wear shorts, I swim naked with you and our pet has a peg leg. Most important, you aren't afraid to touch me, and we make beautiful love over and over again."

"All of that has been inside you. I just opened the door."

"I owe you something else." Preston pulled his cell phone from his pocket and tapped a button to play a prearranged song. He urged her to stand up. "Miss Cindi Pearl Sullivan, may I have this dance?"

"I'd be delighted, Preston James Reynolds."

Wrapped in each other's arms, they moved slowly to James Taylor's "My Romance." *My romance doesn't need to have a moon in the sky.* Preston began to sing with James Taylor, as they moved along the water's edge. The night wind settled, and the frogs ceased their croaking. Even the ducks were drawn to the beautiful sound. *By the way, I can make my most fantastic dreams come true. My romance doesn't need a thing but you.*

"*Hmm,* and he sings too. Again," she murmured, and reached for the bottom of his muscle shirt. "Feel like taking a swim? I'm not wearing any underwear," she confessed with a breathy laugh.

"Minx," he chuckled, and got to work removing her shorts and camisole. "I also want to make love to you on the dock bathed in moonlight."

They'd dispensed with their clothes by the time the song ended a second time. Arm and arm, they made their way down the dock. Preston lowered himself to the boards. Cindi knelt beside his thigh, pressed the release button to remove his simulated leg and slid off the protective sleeve. The first time she'd helped, he was overwhelmed by her eagerness. He was slowly putting a plan together to show her how much he loved her.

Before they slipped into the water, he gathered her in his arms and kissed her until they were both breathless. "I love you, so much."

"I love you too," she sighed, taking an extra breath. He'd fuzzed her brain with that last powerful kiss. She gasped when a sudden splash of night-chilled water hit her in the face.

"Last one in mucks out the barn," he called, treading water.

"You dirty cheater!" Cindi jumped in, dived under the water and bit him on the ass before coming up for air.

"That's how you want to play?" he laughed and slipped his hand between her legs. His fingers teased and sparked the already hot needs of her body. "Wrap your legs around me," he urged, and clamped his lips on the hard nub of her breast. He couldn't wait to make love to her on the dock and slid smoothly inside her.

Yes, yes, his mind cried. He was whole.

At ten the following morning, they met with Judge Margaret Taylor. She'd just removed her judge's robe to reveal a deep, teal blue tailored suit. Around her neck were her beloved pearls, a gift from her late husband. She invited them to sit at the long conference table, bordered by floor-to-ceiling legal tomes. An array of colorful African violets thrived under the sunlight coming in the tall arched window, softening the formality of the judicial office.

Cindi felt half put together. They'd decided to spend the night in their own beds, but she'd forgotten to set her alarm. The orchid shirtwaist was one of her favorites, but she didn't have time to fuss with her hair and had gathered it up in a ponytail. Preston had dressed in one of his proper business suits. He'd forgone his contacts and the sight of him in his sexy glasses helped put her at ease. She reached for his hand under the table.

"Cindi, I've reviewed the complaints, and if it was up to me, I'd bring them in and fry'em, but unfortunately, I have to abide by the law. As a judge, I am required to weigh the evidence to determine a judgment that is fair to you, the victim, and make the felons pay for their crimes. According to Preston's concise report, Mildred Cummings helped herself to money slated for children. Her son defaced your personal property, but there aren't any witnesses or proof he purchased the cans of paint. Security footage shows Harold purchasing the stuffed animal, but we have no proof he was the one who sent it to you. According to Preston's follow-up report, they found utility bills in the garbage. The addresses were not in Webber's sanitation pickup area, so we cannot connect him to the garbage dumped in the barn. If we brought Harold into court, a lawyer would argue that everything is circumstantial, and I would be forced to agree with his representative."

"Whose side are you on?" Cindi challenged, before backing down. "Sorry, Judge. You make valid points and I respect your side of the law, but it sucks!"

"Yes, it sucks," Margaret agreed with an understanding smile.

"Our security cameras caught him the day the package showed up at Adams Security," Preston added. "Harold was driving the garbage truck that picks up the commercial containers in the rear of the building."

Margaret raised a brow. "No package, right?"

"None."

"I know Mildred helped herself to the money," Cindi said, "but I find it hard to believe she encouraged Harold to threaten me and destroy my property. I didn't think there was a spiteful, malicious bone in her body. Look what she's done for her foster children."

"That's why I've been troubled with my findings," Preston said. "Mildred doesn't fit the standard profile of an embezzler. I've also been thinking about Ron. Lincoln has a team that handles gaming theft and fraud. We could talk to Ron and see if he'd be interested working from home for Adams Security."

Cindi leaned into Preston and gave him a quick kiss. "You are a genius!"

"I've got an idea for Carole," Margaret put in. "The town just approved the opening of a new store on the other side of the doggie spa and hotel. Lillian Charles, the chief of police's daughter, is opening a shop featuring local artists. I can put her in touch with Carole to see if she'd like to display her paintings."

The judge's cell phone indicated an incoming text. A slow smile filled her face when she finished reading the message and typed in a reply. "That was Jessie. Mildred Cummings just walked into police headquarters with Harold and demanded he be arrested. I told my daughter to bring them to my office."

"Can I punch him in the mouth for ruining my car and threatening my animals?"

"You'll have to get in line," Preston said. "I protect what is mine."

"No one is going to get physical," Margaret laughed. "When they arrive, I will do the talking and ask Lieutenant Adams to stay as an official police witness. Remember, he can't be officially charged with anything, but before he leaves, I will make sure he pays for what he did to you."

"What about Mildred?"

"I have to give her situation more thought."

Jessie, looking official in her lieutenant's uniform, escorted them into Margaret's chambers. Mildred, a great deal shorter than her bear of a son, was dressed in a black two-piece suit, making the white streak in her hair more prominent. Harold was also dressed in formal black. Before the judge invited them to be seated at the table, Mildred went off like a firecracker.

"I want him arrested for what he did to Cindi Pearl! I'm appalled!" She glowered murderously at her son, who stood stoic with his hands hanging down at his sides. The downtrodden look on his face was that of a little boy who was about to get a switch to his backside.

"I raised him better than that!" Despite the artful application of makeup, her complexion was red from anger. "He confessed this morning about the car, the garbage and threatening you with the stuffed animal. He did it so the derby organization wouldn't go after me for the money I borrowed." She turned to her son and jabbed him in the stomach with her elbow. "Well, what do you have to say to Cindi Pearl? Apologize!"

"I'm sorry, Ms. Sullivan. I hope your animals are okay. I didn't mean to scare them. I couldn't let Ma go to jail. She took us in when nobody cared. It was wrong what I did, but Carole, Ron and I don't know what we would do without her. We love Ma."

"I understand the lengths people will go to when they love someone." Cindi didn't realize the truth of her statement, until the words had left her mouth. Hadn't she been doing that all along for Preston? When his fingers tightened on her hand, she knew he also understood her comment.

Lieutenant Adams addressed Mildred Cummings. "So you admit you helped yourself to the hundred and fifty thousand dollars?"

"Yes, but I'm prepared to replace the money in full. My children are unaware of the stock I inherited from my grandfather. It's been in the family for years, and selling it would have resulted in a big loss. I was waiting for my yearly dividend check before

I put the money back in the account. I never anticipated getting sick." Mildred opened her large purse, withdrew a cashier's check and passed it to Cindi Pearl. "Here is the full amount, plus six percent interest. I know it was wrong to borrow the money, but I needed the extra funds to cover Carole's and Ron's medical expenses and my own. Every year, the dividends covered what I borrowed. I'm just so embarrassed. The board of directors will never want me back."

Cindi was overwhelmed and very grateful for the check in her hand. This mess could finally be cleared up. "Thank you, Mildred. If it will make you feel any better, I never reported the incident to the board, so it will stay in this room. You won't be allowed to handle the treasurer's responsibilities, but we can always use extra hands in other areas. As for bringing in additional funds, Preston and the judge have an idea for Carole and Ron to earn money on their own."

"You are a good person, Cindi Pearl Sullivan, not like my son," she said, giving Harold the evil eye. "I want him arrested."

"Putting him in jail would be the legal thing to do" Margaret said. "There's a strong possibility he would lose his job, creating a big financial hole for you and the others."

"Ma needs my salary." Panic filled Harold's voice.

"I'm aware of the importance of you being able to work," the judge said. "Right now your fate rests with Ms. Sullivan. She'll have to drop the complaints officially."

Do a good deed, for a friend in need, screamed in Cindi's head. She looked to Preston for direction, and he shook his head.

"The decision is yours," Preston said. "Whatever you decide, you have my support."

"Okay, I'll drop the complaints, but Harold can't get away without some type of punishment."

The judge gave Cindi a soft smile. "Putting the needs of others before your own is a rare quality in a person. I will abide by your decision, and punishment will be administered by me."

Margaret addressed Mildred. "Officially you should be charged with embezzlement, but I understand you were thinking of your family. You are very fortunate Ms. Sullivan didn't address this issue with the board of directors. They might have pursued criminal charges. Since you've already included six percent interest in your check, I will eliminate your fine. Officially you will be barred from handling the funds for the derby organization."

She shifted her attention to Harold. "You've already admitted your guilt, but Lieutenant Adams will take your official statement. If it were up to me, I'd throw you in jail for criminal mischief and destruction of private property and tack on a stiff fine. You will pay for the damage to Ms. Sullivan's car and make a five-hundred-dollar donation to the county ASPCA. You will also be required to put in two thousand hours of community service at the Laurel Heights animal shelter. The job includes picking up, in plain English, dog shit."

Cindi lost it and burst out laughing.

CHAPTER 13

Three weeks later, Cindi stood on the top row of the bleachers to get a bird's eye view of the completed Laurel Heights Soap Box Derby Track. It had turned out better than she'd ever anticipated. Rich green grass framed silver metal step bleachers, and white lines denoted the lanes on the black tarmac. A marquee arched over the racing corridor, and colorful banner flags fluttered atop it in the morning breeze. By noon, every seat would be taken, and the first two cars would officially christen the raceway. It was a dream come true, and she didn't know who was more excited, she or the kids.

Once again, the town had shown their generosity in this new venture. The awards ceremony would be held in the open pavilion, courtesy of Whipper Hardware. The beautiful award trophies had been donated by the businesses in Laurel Heights. A number of gift baskets had been given for raffle prizes. She wouldn't mind winning the one from Jojo's Curl Up n Dye that offered an entire spa day. The concession stand would be open for business and the drinks would be free, courtesy of the Spoonful Café. Samantha had baked a slew of cookies that would be handed out to attendees.

The twenty-four derby cars had been stored in the metal storage building paid for by Henry Long and erected by Long Construction. She'd check with the guards earlier, and they would bring the two dozen cars to the starting point by eleven. When her cell phone rang, she reached into the pocket of her jeans, hoping it was Preston. He'd taken the red-eye out of LA and said he'd call as soon as he landed. She missed him like crazy. But it was her friend Terry.

"Cindi, I was hoping to catch you before the race. The specially equipped transport van you sent is perfect. We also got the shirts. The kids are so excited."

"I'm glad you and the Super Kids are going to be here, but I didn't order a special van or send derby shirts."

"Well, it's here. There is also a fifteen-passenger van for parents and handlers. The truck just left with the kids' cars."

Cindi made her way down the metal steps to the bottom. "I'm totally unaware of this game plan."

Some of the enthusiasm faded from Terry's voice. "I got an e-mail telling me about the arrangements. The man also called to confirm pickup times. On top of that, he sent a generous donation to the Super Kids organization. Is the race still on?"

"Absolutely. Did he tell you his name?

"Mr. Smith."

"Smith? I don't know anyone by that name."

"According to the schedule, the Super Kids will be second in the line-up, so we'll see you a little before noon."

"The committee also neglected to send me the change in the racing order. Tell the kids I can't wait to see them."

The moment she ended her call with Terry, her phone rang a second time, indicating a text message. She sighed with happy relief. *Plane just touched runway. Can't wait to hold you in my arms. I love you!*

She texted back. *Hurry. You owe me two weeks of kisses. I am already at the track. I love you, too!*

An hour later, the stands started to fill up. Cindi was getting nervous. Preston still hadn't arrived. She was surprised to see Mildred Cummings and Harold Webber. They'd brought Carole and Ron to the festivities. The bottom row of the bleachers had been eliminated to make it wheelchair-accessible. Mildred held out her hands in greeting, minus her gaudy rings. She'd forgone her flowery dress and paired the neon-purple derby shirt with a long black skirt.

"Here she is! The maker of miracles. Come, I want you to meet my other children."

Mildred's happiness was obvious. "I'd love to meet them," Cindi said.

Carole Gibbons was as delicate as a fairy. Her alabaster-white hair hung loose like a gossamer curtain, and a wide-brimmed hat kept the sun off her delicate facial features. She wore a long flowing dress of soft mint green. The woman was quite beautiful. Ron Tremont displayed a mixed heritage of Asian descent. His ink-black hair was caught up in a short ponytail at the back of his neck. He was quite slender and wore jeans and a derby shirt. Sunglasses hid his eyes, and the brim of his baseball cap shaded his clean-shaven face.

"I am so grateful," Carole began, clutching Cindi's hand with long, slender fingers. "Lillian Charles came to the house.

She loved my pictures and is going to create a special area in her shop just for me. I'm going to be there and featured at the grand opening. This is like a dream come true. Thank you!"

"You are more than welcome, and I look forward to seeing your work."

"I would like to add my thanks," Ron said. "I got a call from Reggie DeWitt, the head computer tech in the Manhattan office of Adams Security. He arranged for the company helicopter to fly me in to their NY office to meet with their cyber game unit. I'm very excited to be working with a great bunch of people." He raised a thick black brow at his mother. "Ma won't be borrowing any more money. My generous salary will cover expenses."

Cindi didn't mention that she'd made all the arrangements, which included a special transport van to pick him up from the airport. "I'm so glad it worked out. You will love working with Reggie and the rest of his team."

Cindi spun around when someone behind her cleared his throat. Harold Webber, dressed in a derby shirt and jeans, twisted his hands nervously. Before speaking, he removed his baseball hat.

"I hope there aren't any hard feelings. I'm really sorry for what I did." He lifted his official nametag suspended by the cloth lanyard around his neck. "I volunteered my pickup to haul the derby cars after the race. Last week, I started my hours at the animal shelter. I really like working with the critters. Ma isn't too happy with me right now. I brought home two kittens, one for Carole and the other for Ron."

"He also adopted the ugliest dog you've ever seen," Ron added with a laugh. "Manfred is a loveable mutt and gets along with the kittens."

The annoying ring of her cell phone interrupted their conversation, and she let it go to message. The number was from the shop that had her VW. She'd been notified a week ago that they were waiting for the special lavender-color paint from the manufacturer, so repairs would be delayed.

After thanking Harold for his help, she headed for the concession stand to get a much-needed cup of coffee and recalled the message. Her heart sank. Today of all days, they were delivering her car at eleven this morning.

"Well, shit!" she muttered, pushing open the side door to the kitchen area of the concession stand. Samantha and Sallie Mae, along with Billy Landis, were passing out coffee, cold drinks and cookies to the race spectators who had come early to get good seats.

"Coffee!" Without saying a word, Samantha passed Cindi Pearl a cup.

"Where is your hunky shadow?" Samantha asked.

"On his way from the airport."

"Ya know, that's funny." Sallie Mae adjusted the bib of her apron, which covered her derby shirt. It was a bit too tight over her very large boobs. "I thought I saw his fancy car the other day going down Main Street."

"Had to be someone else. Preston has been in LA for the past two weeks."

"Well, I could be wrong."

"Speaking of cars, mine is being delivered this morning, so I have to head home."

"Great timing." Samantha avoided eye contact with Cindi and busied herself by placing each large cookie in a clear bag marked with her Tea in Time logo. "Make sure you're back by noon when the first race starts."

"I'll leave now just in case they show up early."

"What do I tell your main squeeze when he comes?"

"I'll send Preston a text and let him know what is going on."

As soon as Cindi left, Samantha gave Sallie Mae thumbs-up, pulled her cell phone out of the pocket of her jeans and hit the speed dial. "She just left." Samantha paused and then followed with, "You couldn't pay me enough to be in your shoes right now."

When the delivery truck failed to show at eleven, Cindi re-called the number on her cell phone. To her frustration, it went straight to message. She still hadn't heard from Preston, so she accessed the personal GPS app on her phone. "What do you mean, access denied? This is nuts!" She called his number and it went straight to message.

She tried to relax in the wicker rocker on the porch. Donut had sensed her anxiety and curled up on her lap. Cupcake, Muffin and Cherry Cheesecake gathered at her feet. Cookie paced the front yard, cock-a-doodle-doing. At eleven-thirty, Donut jumped down and the others went on alert when a flatbed truck pulled down the drive. Pansy sat proudly on the back, beautifully restored. The young driver hopped out of the truck, all apologies.

"Sorry, miss. Your fiancé insisted we ignore our GPS and follow his directions. He also said the delivery had to wait until this morning. We've had your vehicle in our warehouse for a week. He even paid extra for storage."

"Fiancé?" I'm not engaged."

"Well, this guy called our office and identified himself as your fiancé."

"Did he give you his name?"

The driver pushed up his aviator sunglasses and read the manifest in his hand. "Mr. Smith."

Cindi pursed her lips. Again, the mysterious Mr. Smith. Something was going on. "I would appreciate you unloading my car as soon as possible. I have to be someplace, like, an hour ago."

"Nice shirt," he commented. "When I was a kid, I raced in the soap box derby. I didn't know Laurel Heights had its own track."

"They do now. That's where I have to be."

"Give me a few and you can be on your way."

It felt so wonderful to get behind the wheel of her beloved Pansy. Cindi glanced at the time on the dash. The first race would start in twenty minutes. That gave her ten minutes to spare. She'd be cutting it close and decided to go a little faster. Her little car needed the exercise. The sound of a police siren and flashing lights in her rearview mirror put a damper on her happiness. She was being pulled over by one of Laurel Heights' finest on a country road, in the middle of nowhere.

"Patience, Cindi," she whispered as Officer Lynch asked for her license and registration before checking with headquarters. Since she had a clean driving record, he issued her only a warning.

Cindi never saw him reach for his personal cell phone and call Lieutenant Adams to let her know Cindi was on her way to the track.

It was ten after twelve before she got back on the road, furious that she'd missed the opening ceremonies and the first race. Adding to her frustration, all of the parking spaces were filled. Parking was available down the road in the Adams Security parking lot, a quarter mile away!

She parked in her own designated spot and jogged down the newly placed brick sidewalk. Sweat ran down her temples, and her shirt was sticking to her back. When she approached the staging area where only staff, drivers and handlers were permitted, she was stopped by a volunteer she'd never met before.

"Sorry, miss. I can't let you through," the man said.

"You are doing a great job keeping out spectators, but I'm staff." She smiled and reached for her nametag at the end of her lanyard. She looked down. It wasn't there. In her haste to get to the race, she'd left it on the front seat of her car. "I don't need this." She sighed in frustration and searched the crowd. "See that woman over there with the kids in the wheelchairs? She'll tell you who I am. "

"One second," he said with a great deal of skepticism and came back a few minutes later. "She said you're legit. Okay, go ahead."

"Thanks," she said hurriedly and proceeded to the rows of derby cars that were lined up to take their turn. Drivers and handlers mingled close to their respective cars, but cars eight and thirteen, the first two selected to start the race, were still in position. She wondered why the start had been delayed and looked about for one of the other advisors. Not seeing any, she headed for the Super Kids tent.

Cindi wasn't surprised to see Edith Amanda Adams, wearing her derby shirt, in the thick of things, laughing with Belinda as they played on her iPad. Cindi's footsteps slowed when she spotted her missing hunky shadow, chatting with Lincoln and her brother! A slow boil of anger bubbled in her body at the site of Preston's derby shirt. The black T-shirt matched those worn by the Super Kids. A big "A-Team" dominated the front. His included the special numbered account from their secret benefactor. *Liar*, her mind screamed.

Preston sensed his love was near, and the smile on his face died. She wasn't supposed to be in this section. Adams Security guards, dressed in derby shirts, were watching for her lavender car at the entrance to the derby grounds. They were to call him as soon as she was spotted. From the furious look on her face, he was in deep shit.

Lincoln, too, saw his administrative assistant and shook his head. "I sure hope you have a good explanation. You two are supposed to start the race at one o'clock."

"Wish me luck," he said, searching his mind for something to tell her.

Hands clenched into fists, Cindi took a step toward the big fat liar, but a full-of-life ten-year-old ran in her direction and yanked on her wrist.

"Cindi, come meet Belinda. She is special."

It was the distraction she needed to take the edge off her anger, and she followed Edie. She forced a smile and wrapped her arms around the eleven-year-old in the wheelchair. "I am so glad to see you."

"Me too," she smiled, returning Cindi's hug.

"Belinda is my new friend, and her birthday is the day after mine," Edie eagerly stated. "Her mom said it was okay for me to come over to her house and hang out sometimes. And guess what? She plays the piano, too!"

Edith Amanda's exuberance evaporated, and she turned away from her new friend. She needed to get something off her chest and lowered her voice. "Cindi, I know God makes all children, but I don't understand why they aren't all perfect and healthy. Belinda had cancer and lost part of her leg. She can't run around and play basketball and soccer like me. I know God isn't mean, but why would he do something like that?"

The frank and touching question took Cindi totally by surprise, and she blinked back the hot tears that filled her eyes. *Think, Cindi, think.* She recalled they both played the piano and it gave her an idea. She laced her voice with softness and addressed both of the girls. "We don't always understand why God does things or his reason. Children with physical and mental disabilities hold a very special place in God's heart." She took a hand from each girl and entwined their fingers. "Edie, you too, are special, but in a different way. God has guardian angels on earth to help him take care of his special children. Maybe God's plan was to have you two meet at this exact moment so you could become pals. Friendship between two people is very powerful and lasting. Who knows? Someday you and Belinda might play duet pianos at Madison Square Garden."

"Yeah, like Billy Joel and Elton John!" Edie cried.

Her explanation seemed to appease Edie and Belinda, but she still needed answers about the personal mess she was facing She turned and came face to face with the deceiving good-for-nothing.

"That was quite beautiful," Preston said and he braced himself for the storm brewing in her eyes.

She jabbed a finger in the center of the letter *A* on his chest. "This must stand for asshole!"

As usual, her rant drew attention, and he put a hand to her wrist. "Can we discuss this in private?"

She yanked her arm away. "Why? Am I embarrassing you?"

"No, you are embarrassing yourself." Things were going downhill fast. The entire town was waiting for the special race.

Edie Adams had no problem stepping into the fray and clasped Cindi's hand. "Don't be mad, Cindi. He only put the holes in the bathroom wall so you would think there was a problem with the pipes. Mr. Preston needed an excuse to move to the farm to protect you and the animals."

"Who told you that?"

"Daddy and Mommy told me because I missed Mr. Preston. We couldn't play one-on-one anymore."

Cindi glowered at her boss when all he did was offer a tight-lipped smile. Luckily her brother had made himself scarce. As a member of the board, he was probably a part of this farce.

"You all should be given Oscars for your performances!"

"Oh, you have to be in a movie to get one of those," Edie said. Adults were so confusing.

"They were in a movie. It's called *Let's Make a Fool out of Cindi Pearl.*"

Preston took her arm again, using a bit more force. "Let's take a walk and I'll answer your questions."

She didn't budge and studied the numbers on his shirt. "You're the secret benefactor." Before he could reply, she suddenly realized what the numbers represented and jabbed the number four, then fifteen, then twelve with her finger. "Those damn numbers spell out the word *dolphin!*"

"Can't get anything by you, Cindi Pearl." Preston noticed the surrounding crowd was getting larger. They were also wasting time.

"You knew all about derby racing and let me go on and on, explaining everything. 'Oh, Cindi, I'm so impressed with your knowledge of soap box derby racing.' Bullshit!"

While she continued her tirade, he guided her away from their audience and took refuge behind the concession stand, which afforded them some privacy.

"Now, to answer your initial question, yes, I knew about derby racing, and no, I didn't make a fool out of you."

She pulled her arm out of his grasp and struck a belligerent pose against the side of the frame building. "Were you in LA a full two weeks?"

"No." Preston crossed his arms in front of his chest and stood directly in front of her. "I came back last Tuesday and have been staying in the apartment above the garage. In case you were wondering, they replaced the old pipes since I wasn't living

there. It killed me to stay away from you, but it was necessary."
He really wanted to take her in his arms and kiss her until they
were both incoherent.

"Why?"

"I can't tell you just yet."

"So you're the mysterious Mr. Smith."

He gave a slight bow. "Hannibal Smith, at your service."

"Right, from *The A-Team*," she sneered. "How could
I have missed that obvious corny clue? Why didn't you want
me to know you are the one who has been sending us money
every year?"

"I can't tell you just yet."

"Does my brother know what's going on?"

"I can't tell you just yet."

"Why did you have them hold my car for a week and give
the driver crazy directions to the farm?"

"I can't tell you just yet."

"Is that to be your standard evasive answer?"

"For now."

"Why did you fake the plumbing problem at the apartment?"

"I can answer that question. I didn't want you to become
more alarmed if I suddenly moved into the barn apartment, so I
devised the fake plumbing problem. I wanted to be close if there
was any more trouble. Truthfully, I wanted to be close to you."

Cindi tapped a foot in irritation. "Since when did you
become my fiancé? I don't recall you ever asking me to marry
you. Right now, I wouldn't give the question a moment of
my time!"

"I can't tell you just yet." From the way things were going, he was facing a lonely future. How could all of his precise plans have gone awry? Thanks to Jessie, he'd even gotten the cooperation of the Laurel Heights police.

She needed to put a great deal of distance between them and pushed away from the building. "I've had enough of being made the fool and your stupid bullshit answers."

When she started to walk away, he knew of only one way to stop her. "I love you!"

His confession doused some of her anger and shot straight to her heart. She stopped. Hadn't she done things behind his back, all in the name of love? She didn't fight the hands that rested on her shoulders and the familiar hard body pressed against her back. She closed her eyes and breathed in his clean scent, the scent she'd missed and craved these past two weeks. The warmth of his breath swept across her ear, and she melted against his strong chest. "I love you, Cindi Pearl, more than life itself. I've been waiting forever. You've made me whole. Give me a chance to prove that love. All of your questions will be answered if you'll come with me."

CHAPTER 14

He was a lying, conniving jerk, but she loved him. She just nodded.

"I have to blindfold you."

She spun around and jammed her hands on her hips. "You're kidding, right?"

"No," he laughed and pulled his white handkerchief from his back pocket. "I can assure you, I'm not in this alone. It's only a short distance to the reviewing stand." He kissed her pouting lips. "Come on. We've kept everyone waiting long enough."

"Who is everyone?"

"All in good time." He secured the soft cloth in the back of her head and laid his lips on her soft neck. "It will all be worth it, Cindi Pearl Sullivan." He reached for his cell phone. "We're coming," he said when Lincoln answered.

He kept a secure arm around her waist as they walked down the blacktop walkway that led to the hub of the festivities. Voices filled with excitement grew louder the closer they got to the bleachers and reviewing stand filled with town dignitaries. When Preston and Cindi came in sight, everyone started cheering and clapping.

"From the sound of things, everyone knew what was going on but me."

"It wasn't easy with the gossip that flies around this town. We're at the reviewing stand. Go up four steps and don't move until I take off your blindfold."

The moment the handkerchief was removed, Cindi blinked to make sure she was seeing clearly. A huge banner had been erected over the track. "Winner Takes All." Sitting under the arched marquee that designated the starting line, were two derby cars, each big enough to accommodate a single adult. One was freshly painted a sunny yellow and displayed the name Canary in black script letters. The other car was a bright sea green. Supporting the name Dolphin was a surfboard.

"How did you get my car? Dolphin, that's your nickname. Does that mean you raced in soap box derbies?"

"Until I was eighteen. I modified both cars and adjusted the length and weights to accommodate our mature bodies. That's what I've been working on the past few days. As for how I got your car, look." He grinned and nodded toward the bleachers closest to the reviewing stand. Her parents were sitting next to her brother and his family on the third row. They were joined by Jennie Reynolds and an older couple. Preston resembled his handsome father. All were wearing happy smiles and waving.

"I expected the entire town, but why are my parents and your family here?"

"A long time ago, you lost a race at the last minute and were labeled a terrible driver. I thought it appropriate we have a special race to celebrate the opening of the derby track." He swept a hand in front of the reviewing stand. "This was all your idea. Everything you do for others is a gift from your heart. I wouldn't be standing here, whole and hearty, if it wasn't for you. It's time you were recognized for your personal sacrifice and generosity. The kids, the entire town and I thank you, Cindi Pearl." Preston's voice bellowed out of the loudspeaker system, and everyone started cheering.

He gave a nod and all eyes turned to the track. The Super Kids, led by Jasper, made their way to the front of the reviewing stand. Colorful balloons had been tied to their wheelchairs. Those walking had tied the balloons to their wrists. They carried a homemade sign: "Thank you, Cindi. We love you."

Phillip, one of the boys with Down syndrome, walked across the platform holding a bouquet of flowers and a bag. "These are for you, Ms. Cindi, from the Super Kids. We had a meeting and decided to make you part of our A-Team," he said and handed her the gift.

She reached in the bag and pulled out a black T-shirt. "I am overwhelmed." She kissed him on the cheek. "Thank you, all of you," she said, smiling at the Super Kids, who held a special place in her heart.

When Phillip joined his friends, she brought the pale pink petals of a small mountain laurel to her nose. "So this is why you needed to distract me from getting here."

"Yes, I wanted everything in place, including our cars."

"Why didn't you want me to know you were our secret benefactor?"

"When I researched your background, I saw you were heavily involved in soap box derby racing. I did it for you and all the kids. I never wanted any thanks."

"What's the significance of 'Winner Takes All'?"

"This is our race. It doesn't matter who crosses the finish line first because we've already won the greatest prize of all, never-ending love and happiness." Preston slowly knelt down on one knee, reached into his pocket and pulled out an engagement ring. "Cindi Pearl, will you marry me?" .

This day was full of surprises, she decided, staring at the large white diamond surrounded by soft purple gemstones, sparkling in the early afternoon sun. He'd done all this, for her. She ached to give him her answer and have him slip the beautiful ring on her finger, but not just yet. He stood up, unassisted, and she patted his cheek. "I have to think about it. You'll get my answer when we cross the finish line."

The spectators never expected to enjoy a "soap opera" drama before the race, and her comment was met with a mixture of gasps, cheers and whistles.

"You're going to make me wait?" Preston decided that life with Cindi Pearl was going to be fun, full of surprises and exasperating.

"After what you put me through? Oh, and if I beat your time, you'll have to confess to the entire town you surfed bare-ass naked in full view of Mount Saint Elias, Alaska."

Cindi was well aware the loudspeaker system had picked up everything she'd said. She slipped the A-Team shirt over her head and yanked it down before giving him a quick, hard kiss. "Beat you across the finish line!"

Eagerness had her running down the steps, and she headed for Canary. This was the most important race of her life, with the greatest prize of all, a life of love and happiness with Preston, the man of her dreams. "Winner takes all!" she shouted.

EPILOGUE

Cindi stretched her arms above the white sheet and smiled, deciding that would be her new look. Sometime during the night she'd finally fallen asleep wearing the same smile. Just after dawn, a warm breath swept her forehead and soft lips brushed her cheekbone before she returned to dreamland. Had it been only three days since they arrived at the Reynolds' beach house on the shores of the Pacific? Lincoln offered the newly engaged couple the use of the company jet for a well-deserved getaway. Preston wanted to introduce his future wife to Otter Rock, Oregon, where he'd learned to surf and gained his nickname. Yesterday they'd walked hand and hand along the magnificent rocky beach and were entertained by the antics of the otters frolicking in large tide pools. Others sunned themselves on the flat boulders that dotted the shoreline.

She turned on her side and enjoyed the view through the triple French doors that overlooked the vast ocean of white curls dancing atop the deep blue water. A lone surfer stood straight and tall, balanced on the deck of his board. His golden tanned arms, spread wide like an eagle in flight, countered his swaying balance on his way to the sandy beach. A man in his element, enjoying something he'd denied himself for seven years. He'd been hesitant at first, but determined. After wiping out and taking numerous poundings from the epic waves, and he'd achieved success after a few hours. She was so proud of him.

After a long shower, she spread moisturizer on her sunburned skin and dressed in shorts and a camisole. Ocean swimming wasn't her forte, so while Preston surfed, she'd enjoyed the sun on their private beach. She grabbed a glass of orange juice and her tablet before sitting in one of the padded lounge chairs on the sprawling open porch. She relaxed against the cushions and let the cool breeze coming off of the water dry her wet hair.

Even though they were on vacation, she wanted to check her e-mail and wasn't surprised there were over a hundred messages. A half dozen were from Lincoln with information he requested she pass along to Preston. One had her totally confused. It was from a realtor about a bid Preston had submitted on a piece of property. When she spotted a message from Maryann, Preston's mother, she opened it immediately.

Cindi, since my son doesn't leave you alone for more than a minute, I've resorted to e-mail. Bennett and I want to thank you for bringing Preston back to us. He is once again the son we have always love, and we have never seen him happier. Since our children have decided to move to the other side of the country, Bennett and I plan to explore the eastern part of the US. Your mother and I have been e-mailing back and forth, and I would love to talk to you about wedding plans. See you later. Maryann.

Her happiness dimmed when she read the brief e-mail from Samantha. Lincoln needed her to take on an undercover assignment. Cindi was privy to the dangerous situation, and she was scared for her best friend. They'd located the person who almost killed Treig Taylor and Nate Haines, his FBI partner. Sam would literally be putting herself in harm's way.

Cold sprinkles of water on Cindi's legs made her look up, and her smile was back. "I don't have to ask how much you enjoyed the water. Dolphin is in his element."

"The wind is blowing offshore so it makes ideal surfing conditions, and the waves are firing." He paused. "That means the waves are breaking nicely. When we get some time, we'll watch *Point Break*, the movie with Patrick Swayze. The ending was actually shot at Indian Beach, Oregon. Listen to me going on and on," he laughed before lowering his lips to give her a love-filled good-morning kiss. "When was the last time I told you how much I love you?"

"Just before I fell asleep, but I never get tired of hearing you tell me. You were up early."

"I always enjoyed being part of the dawn patrol, going surfing the first thing in the morning."

"Better you than me. Are you hungry?"

Preston took the towel from around his neck and ruffled his hair before tossing the damp cloth on a vacant beach chair. He wiggled his brows. "Not for food, but always for you." He stretched out on the opposite lounge and noticed the magazine on the table beside Cindi's chair. The front cover displayed a naked male model on a beach wearing a prosthetic leg. He glowered at his lady love. "No way! Don't even think about it!"

She gave him an impish smile and offered him her glass of juice. "You have a great body and could pose for a few photos."

"Thanks, but you are the only one who is going to see me in my birthday suit! I will no longer hang eleven—that is, ride my surfboard naked."

"I wouldn't mind." She grinned. "Before I forget, Lincoln sent you a few messages. He spoke to the four guys you went through therapy with, and they love the idea of establishing the Super A-Team Foundation for disabled kids. They're eager to visit children's hospitals to show life can still be rewarding for those who have lost their limbs or need to get around in wheelchairs. Belinda and Jasper are thrilled to be your junior spokespersons."

"That's great. Sparks and Katz work in the Chicago office. Loaner and Lightning work for one of Adams Security's biggest clients."

"When you have time, I'd love to hear how they got those crazy nicknames," Cindi said.

"You'll meet them at our official engagement party, and you can ask them personally."

"There was another message that had me totally confused, about a bid you submitted on a piece of property. Whatever it is, the owner accepted your offer."

There goes my surprise. Preston sat up, pressed the release button on his prosthesis and drew off the protective sleeve. He reached for the towel and wiped off his stump, faking a groan.

Cindi was off her chair in a flash, and she sat on the side of his lounge. Her fingers automatically massaged his shortened limb. "Are you hurt? You're pushing yourself too hard." She didn't fight the strong arms that hooked around her shoulders and drew her to stretch out beside him. "Oh, you," she laughed and lightly punched his solid chest.

"You were too far away, and I need to hold you." He picked up her left hand and kissed her knuckle, just above her engagement ring. "Have you thought about where we will live after we are married?"

Her finger traced the dolphin tattoo on his arm, just below his shoulder. "I hadn't given it much thought, but I really want to stay in Laurel Heights."

"That's fine, because I am purchasing Mr. Rogers's farm."

Cindi's eyes widened in recognition and she sat up. "That's just down the road from Samantha's property. There are rows and rows of fruit trees and a stone farmhouse. Mr. Rogers's orchards produce the best peaches and apples." She threw herself into his arms and squeezed his chest. "I love it!"

"He's been holding out to see if they find natural gas on his property, but it didn't happen. Now he's eager to sell. The house is sound, but needs quite a bit of work on the inside. I'd like to put an addition on the rear with extra bedrooms, baths and an office. The barn needs quite a bit of work, and the old summer kitchen would make a great guest house for when my parents or yours come to visit."

"I'll love living on a farm, and we'll have lots of fruit. Wait until you taste my peach cobbler!" Cindi lowered herself to him and kissed him lightly. "Hmm, salty, but delicious," she murmured, and sampled his lips a second time, taking the kiss much deeper. Her hand wandered down the front of his board shorts, and she wasn't surprised he was already hard.

A low moan escaped him, and he raised his hips to meet her grazing fingers. Her magic hands knew just where to touch him. "I'd love to take you up on your invitation, but if I don't go in and take a shower, we'll be late. My father is a stickler for being on time."

Cindi gave him one final loving stroke and reluctantly removed her hand. "What time are we supposed to go sightseeing?" she asked with a disappointed sigh.

"We're meeting my parents at the marine science center at eleven. My father is eager to give you a personal tour. We'll have lunch and then visit the Yaquina Head Light. Jennie is meeting us at Mo's Restaurant for dinner. They have the best clam chowder."

"Speaking of your sister, Lincoln shared a great e-mail with us. As the new director of the community center, she outlined a plan to add special facilities to accommodate children and adults with physical disabilities. In addition, she is developing programs for disabled children to interact with other children. There will be a special lift chair for the disabled so they can enjoy the in-door pool. Jennie is an amazing woman, and I look forward to her moving to Laurel Heights. We've got to find her a man."

"Don't even go there. She has sworn off a permanent relationship with a man and plans to be single the rest of her life."

Cindi wrapped a leg and arm around her future husband and snuggled against his warm chest. "You had the same idea, but I convinced you otherwise with my love. Jennie hasn't found the right guy, and she just became my new project. 'Do a good deed, for a friend in need!'"

A hearty chuckle rumbled in Preston's chest, and he burst out laughing. God, he loved this woman. His hand reached for the bottom of her of her camisole and drew it over her head to bare her beautiful breasts. They were going to be late, very late.

AUTHOR'S NOTE

Thank you for reading *Winner Takes All.* This book was not on my schedule to be written until next year, but Cindi Pearl, from *Arrest of the Heart*, kept bugging me to get her story out ASAP. So I stopped writing my current WIP. I wanted this to be a fun romance, considering Cindi's happy, do-a-good-deed-for-a-friend-in-need character, but the more I researched the world of wounded warriors, I felt it should be more about Preston Reynolds, my forensic accountant.

Wounded men and women are a special group of people who have made sacrifices in their lives so that we can enjoy our freedom. They blend in with our everyday lives but live with the horrors of mental and physical pain. I interviewed numerous physical therapists, and they related the difficulties family members have accepting what has been done to their loved one. No matter what country you live in, heroes live among us. The next time you see them, take the time to acknowledge their sacrifice. You might want to say, "Thank you for your service." Go to http://www.woundedwarriorproject.org/ to find out more about these unsung heroes.

****

Another group of unsung heroes are Super Kids. They are a group of physically and mentally challenged children who participate in local soap box races throughout the year. Winners from each race advance to the world famous Derby Downs track in Akron, Ohio, for the world championship race. To find out more about these wonderful kids, go to <u>http://nationalsuperkids.org/</u>.

CONTACT INFORMATION

If you enjoyed *Winner Takes All,* please help other readers find this book:

1. Write a review: www.amazon.com
2. Write a review: www.goodreads.com
3. Follow me on Facebook: https://www.facebook.com/judykentrusauthor
4. Follow me on Pinterest: https://www.pinterest.com/jkentrus/
5. Follow me on Twitter: https://twitter.com/JudyKentrus
6. Visit my Web site: Judykentrus.com and sign up for my newsletter.

Meet the other colorful, fun characters in *Winner Takes All*—

ELUSIVE OBSESSION, Book 1. Scott Landis is bored at his surprise birthday party and is looking for an excuse to leave, but changes his mind when the catering staff rolls in a cardboard birthday cake. Julie Keaton is a widow trying to support her two children and brings in extra money working for her sister's party catering business. Find out what happens when the cake is delivered to the wrong birthday party. Fun romance with a hint of suspense.

Elusive Obsession is exclusive on Amazon, .99 cents or Kindle unlimited. http://amzn.to/1EDSkEj

****

MAID TO ORDER, Book 2. Russell Long returns from vacation to find an ad in a newspaper on his desk. "Wanted: Wife, little or no experience. Willing to pay $20,000." The intended joke backfires, and Russell Long is drawn into the scandalous life of Alexis Snow, a former world-class fashion model once framed for smuggling jewelry. Now someone from her past is out to destroy her life, once and for all. Fun romantic suspense.

****

<u>ARREST OF THE HEART,</u> Book 3, Lincoln Adams closed the door on the painful memories of his past eighteen years ago. When a friend from another lifetime calls in his marker, Linc is duty-bound to fulfill his promise. Forced to save a dying town, he uncovers secrets that will change his life forever.

Sgt. Jessie Taylor has worked hard to gain the respect of her fellow police officers and the people of the town she has sworn to protect. When Lincoln Adams returns to Laurel Heights, he becomes a threat to everything she has achieved and loves.

COMING IN 2016
SAMANTHA KINGSLEY'S BOOK

TEA IN TIME
CHAPTER 1

Walk away, just walk away, Samantha Kingsley told herself for the hundredth time as she parked her Harley in one of the white-lined parking spaces of the newly remodeled Adams Security building. More than two dozen spaces were occupied despite it being four o'clock on a Sunday afternoon. When Lincoln Adams, her former boss had called about a highly critical situation, she couldn't say no. Sam didn't need a crystal ball to know what he wanted to discuss.

Right now, her life couldn't have been better. Within the next few months, she'd realize her dream and open Tea in Time, her small bakery and Victorian-themed tea shop in the quaint town of Laurel Heights. She'd been supplying her cookies and pastries to Sallie Mae, the owner of the Spoonful Café, for the past seven months, and the customers were eager to purchase her sinfully delicious baked goods.

Four tall glass doors dominated the entrance that opened into a spacious, modern lobby. Three Adams Security guards manned a horseshoe-shaped reception area twenty-four/seven. A scattering of light passed through a checker-patterned wall of glass blocks that proudly displayed the black-and-silver Adams Security shield.

"Hi, Sam. Bring us any of your great cookies?" one of the guards asked.

"Sorry, Eric, this is an unexpected visit with the big boss. Stop by the Spoonful and I'll treat you to a cup of coffee and a cherry-cheese Danish."

"You're on. You'll have to take the stairs. All the elevators are locked down because they are updating the security status."

"No problem." Sam pushed open a metal door and walked upstairs to the third-floor administrative level. A small panel to the right of the entry door displayed a keypad. She punched in her code and stepped into a space the length of the century-old brick building. All of the windows had been replaced, and decorative skylights had been added to the slanted roof line. She paused to admire the abounding mountains that resembled a Thomas Cole painting of fall in all its red-gold glory. She'd lived and worked in many places during her ten years as an undercover operative with Adams Security, but nothing gave her more pleasure than viewing tree-strewn mountains she now considered home.

She continued down the wide-open corridor to the last office suite in the building. Visitors had to stop at the desk of Cindi Pearl, Lincoln's very efficient admin, before they got to see the head man. Sam already knew Cindi wouldn't be manning her desk. She and Preston, her fiancé, were away for the weekend, discussing wedding plans with her parents.

Lincoln's door was open, and she could see two men deep in conversation on their cell phones. She recognized Nate Haines, the FBI agent. He'd lost weight since she'd seen him almost seven months ago. His shadowy black beard was gone, and he'd trimmed his dark brown hair. Tan chinos and a tailored shirt with fine navy lines was his dress for a Sunday afternoon. Once again her brain shouted, *You know what this is about. Walk away.*

Lincoln Adams smiled when she walked into his spacious office. He, too, had chosen to dress casually, in slim-fitting jeans and a black sweater. The rear wall of smoked glass windows offered a perfect view of the newly remodeled train depot across the road. Two black-and-silver office chairs sat in front of the gray marble–topped desk. One corner displayed a picture of his wife Jessie and daughter Edie on Jane's Carousel in Brooklyn. A smaller frame held a black and white sonogram of his future son or daughter.

"Hi, boss," Sam greeted her friend. She kissed him on the cheek before making herself comfortable on the wide cushioned seat. "I can't get over the number of cars in the parking lot, especially on a Sunday."

He sat in his high-back leather chair and twisted the wedding ring on his finger. He'd been dreading this meeting with Sam, but it couldn't be put off any longer. Lives were at stake. "I thought establishing the office in Laurel Heights would be slow going, but we've got more business than I ever expected, not that I'm complaining. With me flying into Manhattan twice a week, I haven't been able to stop by to view the progress on the tea shop."

"I met Jessie and Edie coming out of the post office on Friday. She's quite large. Are you sure there is only one baby?" Sam winked. "The renovations have taken a lot longer than I anticipated because of all the changes I wanted. The custom-designed glass atrium took the most time, but they will be adding it to the side of the building in another month, weather permitting. Working for Sallie Mae and taking care of the farm animals have kept me busy."

Nate finished his call and took a seat next to Samantha. He'd have to be comatose not to appreciate the beautiful woman with the champagne-blond hair. Her long, lithe body had been poured into black leather pants and a form-fitting biker's jacket. When she smiled, her sapphire-blue eyes glistened like gemstones. But getting involved with a woman was the last thing he needed. Most of the time he felt like shit. His leg and hip were still bothering him. At times he felt like he was a hundred rather than thirty-seven years old. He folded his hands atop his cane. "Sorry, I had to take that phone call."

"I've known you two a long time, and you've got trouble written all over your handsome faces." She brought her long braid over her shoulder and feathered the brushy tip. "What is it?" *Walk away! Walk away!*

Linc rolled a narrow flash drive between his fingers and retrieved a manila folder from the side of his desk. The word "Confidential" had been stamped across the top. "Sam, you know I'd never ask you to do something if I didn't feel we were out of options. Nate, why don't you start?"

"I went back to work a month ago, and I've been assigned to a damn desk for a few more months. You were involved in my previous investigation into the trucking company smuggling illegal booze and untaxed cigarettes. The case is still open, and I'm determined to get these sons of bitches. The wife of the first independent trucker killed reached out to me two weeks ago and asked if I'd made any progress into the investigation of her husband's death. I owe her for coming in initially so we could set up a task force. She claimed her husband took expert care of his truck, and there was no way his brakes had failed. He'd also suspected he'd been conned into transporting stolen cigarettes." Nate's voice took on a somber note. "Two more independent truckers have been killed. The accidents took place in two different states, so they appear to be un related."

Linc reflected on the precarious situations Samantha had worked in as an undercover operative. None were like this assignment. She would be risking her life, and he would never forgive himself if something happened to Sam. He wanted to warn her off, but the decision whether to take on the case would have to be hers. "Nate has come up with an idea."

Her suspicion had been correct, but she remained silent. She crossed her knees and knitted her fingers together. *Walk away, now!*

"His proposal is that you go undercover as an independent driver," Linc continued. "They would never suspect a sassy, sexy woman. A confidential informant working in the company reported Andrew Sayers has moved up in the organization. I personally want that bastard for shooting Jessie when she was a cop in New York."

"Right now the company is experiencing top-level turnover," Nate added. "The founder of the company passed away a few months ago and his two sons, a daughter and a nephew inherited the company. They're also in trouble with their insurance company."

"Adams Security and Investigations has been retained to look into insurance fraud, your specialty. Nate and I wouldn't ask this of you if we thought you couldn't handle yourself. This is a life-threatening situation—yours —so give it serious thought before you take on this assignment."

Sam didn't have to be reminded that Nate and Treig Taylor, Lincoln's brother-in-law, a former agent for the Alcoholic Beverage Control, had barely escaped with their lives. She feathered one of her dangling gold duck earrings with her finger and closed off the part of her brain that advised she walk away. The fee she intended to charge would pay for the equipment in her bakery kitchen and the ornate tables and chairs for the interior of the tea room. "When would I have to start?"

"As soon as possible," Nate said. "The company is currently looking for drivers."

"I have a personal vendetta against Andrew Sayers. I'll need the background info on the owners, accident reports, the info your task force has gathered, any suspects."

Linc passed her the small drive, the folder and a specially programmed burn phone. "Everything you'll need is right here." Lincoln winked, knowing she would understand. "Your handle is the password. I will let the insurance company know our agent will be working undercover."

"I'll need a couple days to get things in order. The construction foreman can oversee the construction on the tea shop. I should be able to live at home, but Cindi and Preston can take care of the animals while I'm on the road. I'll use my own tractor." She gave Linc a confident smile. "Tell the insurance company my fee for doing this assignment is triple Adams Security's fees plus all expenses."

Samantha pushed up from the chair and gave Linc and Nate a military salute. "I'll be in touch."

An hour later, she added a log to the fire in the original walk-in brick hearth before settling in one of the two wing chairs that afforded the perfect spot to absorb the warmth from the dancing flames. The previous owners had attached the former summer kitchen to the rear of the house, creating an inviting, intimate parlor. She'd loved the rental property so much, she'd bargained with Henry Long for the two-hundred-year-old original stone farm house, barn and outbuildings, along with the two-acre pond that Cupcake and Muffin, her pet ducks, used every day.

She savored some of her Earl Grey tea and tucked her legs under her on the wide plaid cushion. The thick manila folder was balanced on her lap. She'd already downloaded the files, but wanted to review some of the paperwork. The top four items were eight-by-ten color photos of the owners of Trans-American Motor Freight. The first two were of an attractive man and woman, Edward and Edwina O'Ryan, thirty-three year old twins. The third picture was of the forty-year-old nephew, Jonathan Ellis.

Her hand trembled when she lifted the fourth picture. The last time she'd seen that compelling, handsome face with the intense green eyes, she was practically naked and was giving him a lap dance.

One year ago

Made in the USA
Charleston, SC
31 October 2015